erilaR

Part III

War God

from the

Sea

erilaR

Part III

War God

from the

Sea

by

Hector Miller

www.HectorMillerBooks.com

erilaR

Part III

War God from the Sea

Author: Hector Miller

Proofreading: Kira Miller, J van Rensburg

First edition, 2021, Hector Miller

Part 3 in the book series erilaR

ISBN: 9798725464139

Contents

Contents (continued)

erilaR – War God from the Sea

"As whom came the army god with the boat here to the Goth's land?"

- Extract from a translation of the Eggja runic flagstone.

Chapter 1 – Gautar (October 471 AD)

(Relevant maps are available on my website.)

Atakam picked his way through the burnt-out remains of Runa's hall, careful to avoid the flame-blackened logs protruding from the ruins like ribs of a long-dead giant. The old shaman shuffled towards the hearth, bent over at the waist, and studied the thick, black marking scratched onto the stone. Thrice he circled the fireplace, then sat down on the ash-covered floor.

He ran a finger across the rune of Ansuz, closed his eyes, and chanted words in an ancient tongue that only the gods could understand. Slowly he brought his dirty hand to his face. He drew breath, inhaling the charcoal dust deep into his being.

For long he said naught. He then issued a guttural grunt, no doubt acknowledging the answer he had received from the gods.

"Ulgin shows the way", he croaked.

Before the shaman could continue, a hulking Hun warrior stepped from the cover of the greenwood. "Boarex has found their tracks", Kursik growled, and gestured with a thumb over his shoulder to an even larger specimen of his race emerging from the mogshade.

"The footprints lead southwest", Atakam said from where he sat beside the remains of the hearth.

Kursik nodded, unsurprised at the revelation of the shaman, and turned to face me. "Fifty warriors carrying much loot", he said. "One man follows them from a distance, watching from the shadows like a wolf."

After I had discovered the destruction of Runaville, I made my way to the hideout of my mentor, Trokondas, only to find his home deserted. Kursik's words reignited the hope that he had not perished in the raid.

Years before, the Isaurian, an exile from the East Roman court, had stumbled upon the broken body of a shipwrecked boy. He had bound my wounds, but before I regained consciousness, he delivered me to the door of the old seer, Runa. For years I lived with Runa and her granddaughter, Unni. The gods intervened and Trokondas became my mentor, teaching me the way of the warrior.

Boarex must have divined my thoughts, and said, "I believe that your friend is the one who watches the attackers."

I noticed then that he gripped something in his fist, but the object was obscured by the tall grass. The Hun nonchalantly tossed a severed head onto the floor of the hall, causing a cloud of ash to rise. "And watch is not all he does", Boarex added. "We found three heads. Close together. Each one taken by a single blow from a sharp, heavy blade."

Kursik gestured to my bearded axe. "He is the one who taught you?"

"Trokondas is his name", I replied.

Boarex rubbed his stomach, glanced at the setting sun, and started down the track towards the beach. "Come", he said. "Let us fill our bellies with meat and fortify our bodies with ale. I wish to die a warrior's death, not starve like a peasant."

We found Sigizan the Hun, Asbadus the Isaurian, Beremud the Goth and Abdarakos, the war leader of the Heruli, seated around a fire. A few paces distant, another fire blazed, surrounded by ten men – the remaining oathsworn of my grandsire.

My eyes searched the nearby shingle beach for the longship of my uncle. Mourdagos, the leader of the Boat Heruli, had brought us to this distant shore after we had escaped the treachery of the usurper Rodolph, who styled himself as king of the Heruli.

"I asked him to leave", Abdarakos growled. "A man's destiny is his own."

The grizzled Heruli took a deep swallow from his ale horn. "A warrior does not fight well when a path of retreat lies open to his rear. We will either succeed in this land, or my brother-in-law will discover our bleached bones when he returns by the last full moon of summer."

"I wish to search for Unni and my friend Trokondas", I said.

Abdarakos regarded me for a span of heartbeats, his grey eyes devoid of emotion. "And what makes you believe that I will allow it?" he asked, his voice suddenly carrying an edge.

My grandsire had not only commanded the armies of the mighty Heruli, but he had also been the favourite of the great khan Attila, overlord of the Scythian and Germani tribes, ruler of the four corners of the earth. But those days were long gone.

In response to his words my hand tightened around the haft of my axe. I felt the anger stir inside, but clenched my teeth in an effort to restrain the beast.

Abdarakos's scarred face broke into a grin, revealing the jest. He slapped my back, clasped my neck in a grip of iron, and pulled me closer, placing his forehead against mine. "I see that the fire of the khan still burns in your blood", he whispered. "I am proud of you Ragnar, you wish to do the honourable thing."

At that moment they attacked.

A screaming warrior ran at me and rammed the tip of his spear into my side. But the thick scale and chain of my East Roman armour turned the fire-hardened wood. Before the man could regain his composure, the flat of my Isaurian axe slammed into his temple, shattering the bone. He crumpled to the ground, falling into the blazing fire and lighting up the surrounds in a shower of sparks.

Abdarakos was slower to react, but not by much. The barbarian's sword did not pierce his liver, but slid off the near impenetrable iron scales. In a stroke of bad fortune, the tip of the blade deflected into my grandsire's face. Abdarakos was no stranger to injuries and ignored the blood that poured from the wound. Grimacing through bloodstained teeth he swung his great sword in an arc, wiping the attacker's parry aside to allow his polished iron to bite deep into the man's skull.

Asbadus, Beremud and the three Huns were similarly assailed, as were the oathsworn. Soon we were surrounded by overwhelming numbers of the foe. Our superior armour, weapons and skills allowed us to keep the attackers at bay, but I realised that we would not be able to hold them for long.

An almighty roar, like that of an enraged beast, erupted from the dark woods behind the savages. A bear of a man, clad in armour, burst from the shadows. His axe moved from side to side in a blur, like the scythe of Hella, the dark one. Seven of the foe succumbed to his iron in fewer than ten heartbeats. They died screaming, blood pouring from the most horrible of wounds.

Even highly trained warriors cannot prevail when assailed from two sides. The rabble who still lived, cast down their spears and melted back into the darkness whence they had come.

* * *

Trokondas removed his gilded iron helmet and spat in the direction of a corpse. "The Gautar are vermin, a despicable people", he sneered. "They are kin of the Goths, who are not much better."

He walked towards me and embraced me in a bear hug. "It is good to see you, Ragnar", he said. "Runa foretold your return."

He then noticed Asbadus, his kinsman, and embraced him as well.

"Do you not greet an old friend, Isaurian?" Abdarakos said and took a step towards us, his face covered in blood.

"Lord?" Trokondas said and went down on one knee before the erilar.

"I owe you a life, Isaurian", Abdarakos growled, clasped arms with Trokondas, and raised him to his feet.

"You can never owe me anything, lord", Trokondas said. "I can only hope to repay a portion of what I owe you."

"Then start repaying me and see to my wound", the erilar said.

While Abdarakos's oathsworn surrendered the corpses of the attackers to the ebbing tide, Trokondas tended to the erilar's wound. The Gautar's sword had not cut deep, but the gash ran all the way from forehead to chin. Worst of all, the blade had cut the eye.

When the wound had been cleaned, stitched and bound, Abdarakos sat himself down beside the fire on the furs and held out his drinking horn. Once all our cups were brimming with golden ale, my grandsire nodded to Trokondas.

The hulking Isaurian wetted his throat and told his tale.

"Two tribes inhabit this land", he said. "To the north live the Svear, to the south the Gautar."

"For many years the Danes, who live across the channel to the south, have preyed upon both peoples. The Danes attack from the sea, raid the villages, and disappear before the local chieftains are able to respond."

"Recently the Danes and the Gautar have concluded a peace sealed by marriage. They refrain from raiding each other's lands and send warriors to aid the other when needed. The raids on the people of this land have intensified since the inception of the peace. It is a dark time for the Svear. Their king, Aun the Old, is no warrior. He remains inside his great hall in Uppsala while the Gautar raze the lands to the south."

My friend and mentor drank from his cup and wiped the foam from his beard with the back of his hand. "The warband came by land a few days ago - fifty Gautar warriors armed with fire-hardened spears. The men and women of Runaville who were not killed were taken."

When I heard of the fate of Runa and Unni, I felt as if the fist of a giant gripped my heart. But then the big man placed a paw on my shoulder. "Hear me out", he said.

He swallowed a mouthful and continued. "The fools fired the village", he said. "The black smoke alerted me to their deeds. I left soon after and followed their tracks which led back to their lands."

"When it was dark, I came upon the Gautar camp. Three of the swine guarded Runa and Unni. I waited until the middle hour of the night and silently dispatched the men keeping watch. After I had separated the captors' heads from their bodies, I fled with the women."

"Where are they, then?" I asked.

"They are at my home", Trokondas said.

His words banished the darkness from my heart. I wished to jump up and run to Unni, but managed to restrain myself.

"And how come you knew that the Gautar would attack us?" I asked.

Trokondas held up an open palm to stall my questions.

"When the Gautar discovered that their fellows had been slain and the women taken, they sent thirty warriors in pursuit. Although we had gained a lead during the hours of darkness, the old woman slowed us down."

"The Gautar are akin to wild beasts", he snarled. "They run without tiring, unencumbered by armour or iron."

Trokondas swallowed the last mouthful remaining in his cup. "I could not risk the lives of the women", he said. "Once they were safe, I led the Gautar away from my hideout. I decided to come to the beach to see if I could find a boat to escape in – if not, I would have made a stand, here on the shingle. But when the Gautar noticed you, their greed got the better of them and they attacked, their courage bolstered by their numbers."

Abdarakos had listened intently to the words of Trokondas and nodded when the Isaurian was through. He came to his feet with a grunt and spoke up, for all to hear. "Ulgin has brought us to these distant shores", the erilar growled. "The god has shown us who our enemies are. Honour demands that we avenge the blood that they have spilled this night. Soon the Gautar will curse the day they took up the spear against the Heruli."

In response to the erilar's words, shouts of agreement resounded to the heavens.

Chapter 2 – Food

I scooped the comely blonde girl into my arms. "I waited for you", Unni whispered, and I felt her warm breath in my ear. "The answer is still 'yes'."

While in the old woman's embrace, I felt her thin frame wrack with sobs. Runa was the mother I never had, and I broke down as well. She slipped from my arms, and like a mother would, wiped away my tears with the long sleeve of her undyed woollen robe.

"Are they tears of happiness?" she asked.

"Yes", I said, "and yours?"

"No", she replied, and fixed me with a hard stare from her rheumy eyes.

"For who then?" I asked, suddenly unsettled.

"Come", she said and turned her back to me, "we will travel to your camp."

I lifted Runa into the saddle, took Unni's hand in mine, and led my horse down the meandering path.

* * *

The sun was low in the sky when we eventually arrived at the beach.

"I wish to speak with the warlord", Runa said, and gestured with her linden walking stick to where my grandsire and the rest of our group sat beside a fire.

Abdarakos was no doubt still in pain from the wound he had sustained the evening before. In the flickering light of the fire, the swollen, purple scar lent a grotesque edge to my grandsire's tattooed visage. Despite his discomfort, he rose from the furs.

Unni and Runa inclined their heads to the erilar.

"May I approach, warlord?" Runa asked.

A frown creased my grandsire's forehead, and in that moment I feared that he would issue a rebuke. But to my surprise he nodded, assenting to her request.

Runa came to a halt before the intimidating man. In a surprising display of familiarity, she extended a wrinkled hand and placed it against his scarred cheek.

"You will lose the eye", she said, and I gave him her words. "In return for your sacrifice, the gods will grant you wisdom."

Seemingly satisfied, she withdrew her trembling hand, inclined her head in respect, and retreated.

* * *

Soon the harsh winter of the north would be upon us. A stout oak hall was a necessity we could ill afford to go without.

Early the following morning, Trokondas, Asbadus, Beremud, Boarex and I ventured into the forest to fell trees. We wore no armour and left our sword belts in our tents. But fools we were not. Sigizan and Kursik kept pace with us, hidden in the shadows, their arrows nocked to the strings of their horn bows.

While we toiled in the woods, Abdarakos and his men accompanied Runa to the nearby villages in an attempt to gain supplies for the winter. The erilar had brought his treasure with him from Moravia. I knew that the lure of gold and silver coin would be too great a temptation for the local villagers to resist.

During the days that followed we had little time to dwell on thoughts of revenge. First, there was another foe to vanquish – the terrible winter of the north. Our time was spent felling trees, digging holes for the great oak posts, and hunting what little game

13

remained. In the evening we huddled around fires before succumbing to fatigue.

By the time the interminable snow arrived on the back of the northerly gales, we sat around the fire that blazed in the hearth of our new hall, sharing food and mead we were able to procure or gather.

We did not have the option to hunt as the animals were long gone, having taken refuge in the depth of the far-off pine forests. When the second month of the new year arrived, we were scraping the proverbial barrel.

"You do not seem concerned about our lack of food, woman", Abdarakos observed one evening, early in the second month of the new year.

"This year there will be no famine", she said. "The time of the great gathering, the *Disting*, approaches."

Abdarakos stared at her quizzically.

"It is the great *Thing*, the assembly of all Svear", she said. "Every eighth year, the *Disting* takes place. Representatives from all corners of the land meet to make decisions of importance. Merchants take advantage of the gathering and arrive with wagons loaded with goods and produce. Sacrifices are made to the gods to seek their blessing of the coming planting season."

"Where?" he asked.

"Uppsala, the home of the king", Runa replied. "And I will be travelling with Ragnar. Join us if you wish."

* * *

Two weeks later we departed – Abdarakos, Atakam, Trokondas, the three Huns, Asbadus, the two women and me. During the harsh Northern winters, the days were short and the nights long, so we set off early, with the sun yet to rise.

Abdarakos and Atakam were mounted, as were the three Huns, who viewed travelling on foot as an insult of the worst kind. Unni and Runa shared a saddle. Six horses were all we had, leaving the rest of us with no choice but to trudge through the half-frozen muck. All ten of my grandsire's men remained to guard our hall.

Later that day, when the sun hung low in the sky, I noticed Abdarakos lean over to speak to Sigizan. "Take Boarex and Kursik and ride ahead", the erilar commanded. He lifted his heavy pack from the back of his horse and passed it to the Hun. "Take what you need and set up camp five miles down the road."

The three Huns were still gathering our baggage when the bright yellow orb rose above the pine tops. The waxing moon allowed us to travel safely, although it helped naught to dispel the terrible cold that descended on the land after sunset.

I was nearly frozen stiff when we staggered into camp in mud-caked boots. The Huns, who had earlier pitched the tents, took care of the horses, allowing us the opportunity to thaw our tired bodies beside the blazing fire.

"Tell me of the king, woman", Abdarakos said and held out his drinking horn, which Atakam filled with warm ale.

Runa nodded, but waited until she also held a steaming cup. "King Aun is a pathetic creature", she said. "His death is long overdue."

Runa did not mince her words – a trait she shared with the Heruli and the Huns. None replied, but gave the old seer time to provide an explanation. I did not fail to notice a ghost of a smile playing around the corners of the erilar's mouth.

The medicine woman took another swallow and continued. "He is an old fool, bedridden with age", she sneered. "Aun has even outlived his sons. Well, all but one. There is a dark rumour that he had them killed so he could keep the crown for himself."

16

"You should have his throat slit", Abdarakos advised. "Seeing that he is not man enough to do it himself."

Runa did not offer words in reply. The old woman nodded absentmindedly. Her dark gaze, fixed somewhere in the flames, discouraging further questions.

Once we had filled our bellies with grilled meat, we crawled inside the tents and covered ourselves with thick furs. As a trade-off for being allowed to ride, the three Huns took turns to feed the fire throughout the night.

On the morrow the cold woke me, denying the Huns the opportunity.

Sigizan sneered when I complained about the chill. "In the lands of the Huns this is considered mild weather. We would not have survived this night on the Eastern Steppes. I remember, as a boy, that after a cold night we found entire flocks of sheep frozen stiff." He gestured to our Hun horses. "See, they are not even bothered by this."

The Hun passed me a cup of hot salted milk. "Drink", he said. "It is an old trick of the Sea of Grass."

After we had broken our fast on thin oat gruel, we set off.

I had long since informed Trokondas of the happenings at the Byzantine court while I served in the Isaurian guard. I had told him how Aspar, the Gothic general, died by my hand, and how Trokondas's own kinsman, Zeno, had betrayed us. Many times I noticed that he was deep in thought, no doubt thinking about the message from his brother, Illus, who wished for him to return to the Great City of Constantine.

"Have you decided?" I asked, walking beside him down a gentle slope.

Trokondas answered with a question of his own. "What do you think of the Byzantine court?" he asked.

"It is a nest of vipers", I said. "One cannot trust even a single word spoken. Everyone has a hidden agenda."

"Yet you still draw breath", he said, then gestured at the sword, axe and dagger attached to my belt. "And you carry weapons and armour even the gods are envious of. You have been taught the way of the sword and you have become a master of the axe. Altogether, Ragnar, I would say that the Great City did not treat you badly."

I thought on his words. When we reached the bottom of the decline, I said, "You speak true. Does it mean that you yearn to return to the City of Constantine?"

"That, Ragnar", he said, "is for the gods to decide."

Chapter 3 – Disting (February 472 AD)

We travelled north for three more days.

Trokondas and I shared a chuckle when we passed the dilapidated hall of the old ferryman who, all those years before, had tried to murder us. The rivers were all frozen solid and passage was not required.

The closer we came to our destination, the more travellers crossed our path. All were making their way north, towards Uppsala. Most pulled their carts and mules to the side of the road to allow us to pass. The peasants bowed their heads in supplication, not wishing to risk the ire of the strange mounted warriors.

Runa pulled her horse alongside Abdarakos's stallion and motioned for me to give him her words. "How do the Heruli rid themselves of leaders clinging to power?" she asked.

"When a warrior cannot hold a sword in his fist, he is no longer fit to lead his people", the erilar growled. "It matters not whether the cause is sickness or old age – either way, it is an affront to the gods for such a man to draw breath."

"Which god?" she asked.

"Ulgin, the one who is without beginning or end", he replied and his hand went to his wolf amulet.

"What happens to a man who cannot hold a sword?" she asked.

Abdarakos took a swallow from his aleskin and continued. "He is laid upon a great pile of wood where his veins are opened. The pyre is lit and the flames purify his being. Then his shade ascends with the smoke, travelling across the bridge of stars to the land of the gods, where it remains for all eternity."

"And if the man is unwilling?" she asked.

The erilar sneered and spat to emphasize his words. "What man will choose a life of infirmity over an eternity in the company of the gods?"

"How is a man of consequence buried in your lands?" she asked.

"When his shade has been set free by the flames, what remains is collected and interred in the soil together with all that he needs in the afterlife", Abdarakos said. "On top of this, a great mound of soil is raised to ensure that he is remembered."

"What does he need in the afterlife?" she pressed.

"The same that he required in this life", he answered. "His wife, weapons, armour, horses and an ale horn. What more does a man need?"

Runa nodded her thanks and pulled on the reins, allowing Abdarakos to outpace her.

* * *

Late afternoon on the third day on the road, we arrived at Uppsala, which was little more than a collection of longhouses surrounding a large hall. The main building was situated on the flat summit of a hillock in the shade of a giant ash. Apart from a grove of ancient oaks at the western base of the hill, the trees had been cleared to make way for fields.

To the east of the hill, on the flat ground beside a stream, a multitude of people were setting up camp. On the snow-covered field on the far side of the stream, traders, craftsmen and farmers vended their wares and produce from atop laden wagons.

We started towards the camping site, but Runa stopped us and pointed to the trees. "We will stay apart from the people", she said. "Close to the sacred grove."

Once we had found a suitable site, Runa took Unni by the arm. "Come, child", she said, "there is much to be done. I must attend the gathering."

She hesitated for a moment, then turned to face my grandsire. "Will you come to me when I send for you, warlord?" she asked.

Abdarakos grunted his assent, but took the old seer aside. The erilar was no fool, and I was sure that in exchange for our assistance he would require recompense.

When she passed me, she whispered, "And make sure your armour shines like the rising sun. All depends on it." She held my gaze for a moment to emphasize the gravity of her plea.

I sighed, then nodded – robbed of the opportunity to explore the wares in the market.

When Unni and Runa had gone, Beremud sniffed the air, the easterly wind carrying the aroma of cooking fires from the market. He rubbed his stomach and said, "Maybe it is time to sample the local fare."

Atakam sat down beside the fire, cross-legged. He rummaged through his pack, producing a small pot containing a mixture of lard and fine sand. "Erilar, your armour", he said.

Abdarakos did not question the intentions of the shaman. He unstrapped his scale armour, which had been dulled by the journey, and passed it to Atakam. Sigizan sensed the mood of the holy man, and joined him beside the fire with a small amphora of vinegar.

Soon, all except Beremud had followed suit.

"There are more important things than your stomach, Goth", Atakam growled while rubbing the iron with vinegar to rid it of rust.

His words drew a scowl from Beremud. "Like what?" he asked.

"Obeying the gods, for one", the shaman responded, which served to wipe the scowl from the big Goth's face. With a sigh, he joined us.

By the time the sun had set, we were still toiling. I was softening my sword belt with neatsfoot oil when Unni arrived with a woven basket filled with smoked joints of pork, hardboiled eggs and rounds of cheese. Behind her trundled a man carrying a large clay vessel. He eyed us warily, placed the jug at his feet, and scurried off.

When we had drunk and eaten our fill, a man came to summon Abdarakos to the gathering. "The priestess calls for the warlord", the stranger said in the tongue of the Svear.

Abdarakos rose to his full height, his armour shining with the brilliance of a god. He took his famous helmet in both hands and slipped it onto his head. The priceless piece of armour had been a gift from Attila himself. The thick iron plate was fastened to silvered cross-bands with double rows of rivets. Atop the central band sat a golden crest fashioned in the image of a boar.

My grandsire clasped his battle-axe by the gleaming, whetted blade, and slipped it into the loop attached to his broad red leather belt. As was his habit, the erilar rolled his massive shoulders to ensure that his movement was not restricted, then turned to face the messenger.

The man staggered backwards, his eyes wide with fear.

We fell in behind the erilar, all of us towering above the Svear, who looked to be close to losing his nerve.

"Take us to the gathering", I said in an attempt to keep the man from darting into the night.

In response, the Svear swallowed and nodded before leading us deeper into the grove. Eventually we came upon a clearing where twenty people were gathered around torchlight, seated on furs. One of them was Runa.

The old seer slowly gained her feet with the help of her linden stick. "Warlord", she said and inclined her head.

"Give him my words, Ragnar", she said, and continued.

25

"King Aun is clinging to power", she said. "He has informed us that tomorrow he will sacrifice his only remaining heir in the hope that the gods will extend his life."

Patiently Abdarakos listened to her words. He stood as motionless as a statue hewn from rock, the torchlight reflecting off his brandished armour.

She turned to face the gathered elders who still regarded our group with wide eyes. "He is the one who commanded the armies of the god-khan, the ruler of middle earth", she said. "The gods have brought him to this far shore to give us their words."

She gestured for the erilar to speak.

"The old man must die", Abdarakos growled and his hand went to the pommel of his sword.

The rumbling of distant thunder reached our ears and a sudden breeze threatened to extinguish the torches.

"The gods have spoken", Runa croaked, her voice resonating in the complete silence of the grove.

All gathered mumbled their agreement.

Runa turned to face my grandsire. "When?" she asked.

"Now", he said and gestured for her to lead the way.

Chapter 4 – Aun the Old

Twenty-four hearthmen guarded the king. They gathered at the top of the broad stairway that gave access to the raised walkway surrounding the hall. The Svearmen wielded iron-tipped spears, their bodies protected by polished boiled leather. Surprisingly all wore iron helmets.

"State your business", their leader growled.

Runa came to a halt ten paces from the bottom of the stairs. "Tell the king that the elders of the tribe are here to speak with him", she said.

"Return to your tents", the captain of the guard replied and flicked a hand in a gesture of dismissal. "The king will speak with no one before the sacrifices have been made. Once the gods have been appeased there will be more than enough time for talk."

Abdarakos placed his hand on Runa's shoulder and guided her to the rear. "Time for talk is long gone", he whispered. Three times I heard the familiar sound of a horsehair string slipping into a notch.

When Runa stood with the elders, my grandsire drew his sword and took his battle-axe in his left hand. "Let us settle this", he said.

The eight of us formed a line, standing shoulder to shoulder.

"You are outnumbered three to one", the leader of the king's guard sneered. "Leave or die."

Before he had time to draw another breath, a broad-headed Hun arrow slammed into his helmet, splitting the iron and skewering his skull. The corpse tumbled down the stairs and, with a dull thud, came to a rest in the mud.

The remainder of the guards, emboldened by their numbers and angered by the death of their kinsman, surged down the steps with spears levelled. Six of the hearthmen fell to Hun arrows before they closed with us.

I held my bearded axe in a middle guard, the haft parallel to the ground. My right hand gripped the wood near the butt while my left hand was close to the blade, protected by the iron of the beard.

A big Svear attacked me at a run, his eight-foot spear held in an underhand grip, drawn back over his shoulder. There was no need to overdo it when facing a novice. When he had committed to the killing strike and his spear surged towards my chest, I stepped forward with my left foot, and using the haft of my axe as a staff, guided the spear past my body. In the same movement, I rotated my hips and allowed my left hand to slide down the haft.

The blunt end of my axe came around and slammed into the side of his helmet. The dead man's momentum carried him forward for another few steps before he fell facedown in the mud.

I had no time to dwell on my victory – another Svear attacked. My bearded axe whirled through the air. The razor-sharp blade slammed into his chest, sliced through his leathers, and threw the corpse backwards onto the stairway.

There were no more enemies to face, and I glanced to the left. Trokondas's axe descended like lightning and took the head of the man facing him – the last of the hearthmen. To my right, Beremud was prying the blade of his battle-axe from a guard's neck, his foot on the man's helmet for leverage.

"You have deceived us all, Runa", I heard an elder hiss in the local tongue. "These are no mortals. Who but the god of war himself have come with the boat to the Svear's land?" He turned to face the others. "Look", he said, "twenty-four of the best of the king's hearthmen lie dead, while these warriors bear no wounds. Not even a scratch. Look at them – they shine like the gods and have no fear of men."

Runa did not refute the claim, but neither did she corroborate it.

Before the elder spoke again, Abdarakos waved us forward. We picked our way up the corpse-strewn steps with the elders following close behind. My grandsire pushed open the unguarded door.

Two fires burned inside the great hall. Beside the central hearth, Prince Egil, last heir to the throne, stood in only a loincloth. His body was being oiled, no doubt in preparation for the sacrifice. I had expected the prince to be a young man, but he must have seen forty summers.

On the far side, beside the second hearth, an old greybeard lay on a bed, propped up by a multitude of pillows. A slave held the narrow end of a horn to his lips. White liquid, spilling from his toothless maw, dripped from his beard onto the bed.

"I heard rumours that he sucks milk from a deer horn, like a babe-in-arms", Runa said.

My grandsire's face morphed in disgust. "So that is the man who wishes to kill his own son", the erilar growled. He drew his jewelled dagger and strolled towards the king. The slave scurried off, dropping the horn and spilling milk all over the floor.

King Aun cleared his throat to speak, but my grandsire clasped his hand over the old man's mouth and drew the blade across his throat.

"It is the will of the gods", Abdarakos said when King Aun had stopped struggling. The erilar chose his next words carefully.

"Tomorrow we will bury him the old way to ensure that his shade ascends to the realm of the gods. We will raise a mound so that the king will be remembered for all eternity."

While I gave the elders his words, Abdarakos walked towards the prince, who staggered backwards in fear. The erilar grabbed Egil's hand and raised it in the air. "Long live the king", he said, clapped him on the back, and sheathed his dagger.

Outside the door of the hall the erilar paused and turned to me. "You fought well, Ragnar", he said, "but your work is not yet done. Take Beremud, Boarex and Kursik and guard Egil this night. There might be some who see opportunity in the midst of chaos. I will send for the shaman to prepare the body of Aun."

"I left the City of Constantine because I was weary of being a nursemaid", Beremud sighed when I told him of Abdarakos's instruction. "But the spinners of fate are fickle bitches. And besides", he added, his gaze drifting over my shoulder, "I am hungry and thirsty."

For the first time I noticed that the table close to the central hearth was stacked with platters of pork and mutton, freshly baked bread, rounds of cheese and jugs filled with ale.

"The last meal of the prince", Kursik observed, then plonked down heavily on a chair. Using his teeth, he tore a large piece of pork from a steaming joint. Beremud and Boarex followed suit.

In addition to the loincloth, a shivering Prince Egil now wore an expression of horror. I pried the helmet from my head, picked up a soft fur, and draped it around his shoulders.

"Pass the ale", I said, and Kursik handed me a jug and a horn.

While I filled the ale horn to the brim, I gestured for the prince to take a seat beside the hearth.

"Drown your troubles, prince", I said, handed him the horn, and joined my friends at the feasting table.

By the time Atakam arrived, Egil, who had been following my advice with gusto, was crying like a babe.

The shaman raised his eyebrows. "Grief for his father?" he asked.

"Tears of joy", Kursik suggested.

"Because he is to be king?" Beremud asked.

"It's not that", Kursik confirmed. "It's because the old man, not him, got his throat slit."

Atakam took in the scene and his eyes glazed over, as if the gods allowed him a glimpse through the veil of time. "Soon Egil will forget what we have done for him", the shaman said. "All that he will remember is that we killed his father."

Kursik drew his dagger and rose from his chair, his gaze fixed on Egil.

Atakam waved him back to his seat. "Are you a god, Hun?" he sneered. "Do you wish to intercede on our behalf?"

Kursik shrugged noncommittally, then rammed his blade into the tabletop. "Tell me if you change your mind, holy man", he said, and downed the last swallow from his horn.

Chapter 5 – Mor

By the time the body of the old king lay atop the man-high pile of wood, the happenings of the night before were known to all in Uppsala. Many times, the story of the slaying of Aun's guards were retold. Each time the tale became more fantastic. I heard an oldster give an eyewitness account of how Abdarakos alone faced twenty-four men - how my grandsire slew them all with a single bolt of lightning. Two others swore to have seen the same.

"Who are these strange warriors?" the people whispered. "Are they men or gods?"

No matter the answer, it was clear to all that the gods of the strangers were gods of war. How else would one man have been able to slay twenty-four?

Unlike the Christians in the lands of Rome, the ones who followed the old gods had no qualms about honouring new, unknown deities. Especially if the gods were as powerful in war as those the strange horsemen owed fealty to.

When darkness arrived, all gathered for the send-off of the king.

When everything that Aun would require in the afterlife was laid out beside his body, Atakam climbed the makeshift wooden ladder that leaned against the stack. Chanting the sacred rites, he emptied a small amphora of oil onto the corpse and grave goods.

When he stood beside the prince once again, the shaman nodded to Runa, who after honouring the gods of the Svear, thrust a flaming torch into the pyre. Soon, thick black smoke safely guided the shade of the king away from the underworld into the night sky. From there it would find its way across the bridge of stars to the land of the gods.

With Aun's shade having departed on its final journey, there was still something that needed to be done before the sacrifices could commence - the Svear needed a new king to preside over the ceremony.

* * *

Clear blue skies greeted us the following morning, although the thin winter sun did little to dispel the terrible cold. In an attempt to warm myself, I sat beside the fire, breaking my fast on thin oat gruel mixed with goat milk.

I noticed Runa and Atakam in deep conversation twenty paces distant. At that moment the old shaman met my gaze. Using his chin, he gestured for me to approach.

"Take the girl and two horses, I have a task for you", Atakam said, and explained what he wished us to do. "It must not be touched by the sun", he added.

"Unni must be the one to find it", Runa said. "Her blood is of this land."

I nodded in response, but it was not enough for the seer.

"Swear it", she said, and took my hand in hers.

"I give you my oath", I said, which seemed to satisfy her.

Not long after, Unni and I rode from camp, heading east into the woodlands.

"Will you return to the Romans?" Unni asked after we had been riding for a while.

"I never wanted to leave these lands", I replied. "But the gods had other designs. Who knows what they have in store for us?"

"You have not given me an answer, Ragnar", she said.

"I wish to make a life among the Svear and ..." I was interrupted by a deep-throated growl emanating from the undergrowth to the right of the track.

We both reined in. I slipped my axe from its case and Unni took her dagger in her hand.

Less than ten paces away, underneath a rocky overhang, two enormous wolves, a black and a grey, were fighting for supremacy. So focused were they on each other, they paid us no heed. Mesmerized, Unni and I stared at the large males, snarling, biting and rolling in the undergrowth. Eventually the younger grey managed to sink its canines into the throat of the black. With a feral ferocity the wolf ripped open the jugular of its rival. For long the victorious male circled the black until its breathing grew still. The grey then glanced in our direction, bared its fangs, and melted into the undergrowth.

Unni dismounted and approached the black wolf whose lifeblood was seeping into the earth. I wished to stop her, for fear that the animal still lived, but I was too overawed by what we had witnessed.

She bent down and kneeled beside the dead animal. "He must have been the ruler of these lands for long", she whispered and stroked the large scarred head. "But the old must make way for the new. Such is destiny", she added, and I thought I noticed a tear roll down her cheek.

I dismounted as well, to comfort Unni in her sudden sadness. When I stood beside her, I realised for the first time that the dead wolf lay upon a large, flat stone.

The overhang shaded the blood-stained surface from the sun. With the help from the gods, Unni had chanced upon what we had been searching for.

* * *

Later that evening I sat beside Atakam, who had requested my presence. He glanced up at the waxing moon before cutting away the strips of hide which kept the wrapping of furs in place around the stone. Earlier, when six of us had struggled to lift the rock onto the back of a wagon, the old shaman had insisted to wrap it.

He ran his hand across the rough surface, still stained red with the blood of the wolf. "Never should the light of the sun touch it", he said, and removed a bronze chisel and matching hammer from a leather pouch. "Neither must it be scorched by iron", he added.

Under the silver-blue light of the moon, as if guided by a higher hand, the chisel seemed to take on a life of its own as it danced across the stone.

When he was done, Atakam leaned in to inspect his handiwork. He gently blew the dust from the last of the engravings. "Behold the runes of destiny", he said, and fixed me with a sidelong glance. "The ancient stone of the Svear now bears the whispers of the old gods of the Sea of Grass. Now the gods of our people will have a say in the fate of this land."

I heard a shuffle behind me. It was Runa.

"May I?" she asked Atakam.

The shaman nodded. "None must lay a hand on the stone when a waning moon is travelling across the heavens", he said. "But this night, while the moon is growing, it is safe to touch."

After I had given her his words, Runa kneeled beside me and placed both hands upon the engraved stone. "It came from the damp earth in the dark woods", she said. "It is as much a part of this land as I am. Henceforth the Svear will know it as the stone of *Mor*, the kingmaker."

* * *

39

That evening, on the last day of the waxing moon before the winter equinox, the Svear gathered.

The elders, who had come from the far corners of the land, decided who would rule. They were the ones who had rejected the continuation of Aun's reign, the ones who had chosen his last remaining son, Egil.

But King Aun had had other ideas. Were it not for the intervention of the Heruli, Aun would have clung to power. The reward that the Heruli demanded was to be allowed to settle in the lands controlled by the Svear. In addition, their warlike gods would be accepted alongside those of the tribe. But most important of all, through the stone of *Mor*, they would have a say in who wore the crown.

Runa and Atakam presided over the ceremony. Once the gods had been appeased and the people content, Egil was lifted onto the sacred stone, from where he made his oaths to the gods of the Svear and the Heruli.

Chapter 6 – Recompense

The following day, on the night of the full moon, the king of the Svear presided over the offerings. Male animals, anything from horses to chickens, were sacrificed. They were strung up on the branches of the ancient oaks in the sacred grove so that their lifeblood could soak into the earth to appease the gods. The shades of the victims would live on, joining the life force of the trees and strengthening the power of the grove.

For nine days the sacrifices continued unabated to ensure a good harvest and to guarantee victory in war.

When the gods' appetite for blood had been sated, a steady stream of peasants, merchants and farmers started to trickle out of Uppsala. They were eager to get back to their huts, halls and families. When our own loaded wagons creaked under the weight of the grain, meat, ale and cheese, Abdarakos was summoned to attend the king. In order to bridge the language divide, I joined the erilar.

Egil, flanked by his newly appointed hearthmen, met us at the bottom of the steps leading up to his great hall. It was clear that the king had put the shock of the past few days behind him and had managed to come to terms with his newfound good fortune.

Neither I nor Abdarakos bowed before the king, and I noticed a look of disapproval in his eyes. But it was gone in less than a heartbeat.

He embraced Abdarakos and me in turn. "Truly, the gods have sent you to me", he said. "My life and my kingship I owe to you. I have agreed to the request of the elders. You will be allowed to settle in my lands."

"Over and above that", Egil added, "is there anything I can help you with?"

"There is", Abdarakos replied. "At the next full moon, send thirty spearmen south to Runaville – we have unfinished business with the Gautar."

My grandsire's answer pleased Egil, who struggled to contain his emotions. "It seems that our goals are aligned, Lord Abdarakos", he said with a grin. "I will do as you ask."

We both touched our foreheads with our right hands in the way of the people of the Sea of Grass, which Egil acknowledged with a nod before we departed.

* * *

On our way home we were blessed, or maybe cursed, with pleasant weather. We thanked the gods that we could still cross the frozen rivers, but the ice was melting. Travelling with the heavily loaded wagons proved to be a challenge. The oxen struggled up the slopes, with the narrow wheels of the wagons cutting deep into the muddy mire like the shears of a plough, requiring us to push from behind. Twice I slipped and ended up facedown in the mud. On the downhills, the wagons tended to veer to the side as soon as the rim brakes were applied. More than a dozen times the Huns saved the day by pulling the wagons back onto the path using their lassos.

The first night on the road I collapsed onto the furs after pitching my tent. I slept through the evening meal, only waking up early the following morning when Kursik kicked my leg.

My sinews were stiff from the toil of the day before. Kursik extended his hand, pulled me to my feet, and gestured that I should follow him to the cooking fire.

The Hun passed me a cup of warm ale, a joint of smoked pork and a round of soft cheese, then sat down cross-legged on the furs.

He took a swallow from his cup. "You should take the girl as your woman", the Hun growled. "Or, if you don't want her, let me know", he added, and eyed me over the rim of his cup.

"Leave her be", I said. "Or do you wish to come between the son of the khan and his woman?"

Kursik stood, and a sly smile played around the corners of his mouth. He placed his hand on my shoulder. "I would never dream of it, Ragnar. But I have seen you charge into battle without a thought for your own safety, but when you are in the company of Unni …", he said, and shook his head wearing a resigned expression.

"I will speak with her when the time is right", I said.

The Hun grunted something incomprehensible, waved away my words, and left to tend to his horse.

* * *

The remainder of the journey to our hall was challenging but without incident.

We had sufficient food to see us through the winter. Runa had made sure that Abdarakos purchased enough seed to sow the fields come the planting season. In addition, a long train of cows, goats and pigs trailed behind the wagons. Although there was no shortage of food, the raid of the Gautar had robbed Runaville of its inhabitants. There was a dire need for farmers to cultivate the land.

But there was also another need – one that eclipsed the need for the return of the people. It was the desire for revenge. Therefore, it came as no surprise when Abdarakos raised the issue on the first evening after our return.

The erilar sat opposite me, on the other side of the hearth. He wore a tunic only, but the thick, soft fur of a brown bear was draped around his shoulders for warmth.

He gulped down the remainder of the mead in his cup and wiped the golden juices from his beard with his sleeve. "You were tutored by a Greek, Ragnar", he said and held out his cup for a refill. "Tell us what the Greeks, the learned men, say about revenge."

"They say that a man of weak character is easily offended", I replied. "Such a man seeks revenge, which leads to an endless cycle of violence."

"And what do you say, Ragnar?" my grandsire asked.

"We should attack the village that sent the warriors who had razed Runaville", I suggested. "But more than that, we must destroy all the villages in the vicinity."

"Why?" Abdarakos asked, a frown furrowing his brow. "Is it to put the fear of the gods into their hearts, so that they will refrain from attacking us again?"

For long I thought on the words of my grandsire, searching for a truthful answer. "No", I said at last, "that is not the reason."

The old warrior did not speak again. His frown disappeared and his blue-grey eye bored into my soul.

"I wish to attack the Gautar to sate my thirst for revenge", I growled. "I wish to make them suffer like the people of Runaville suffered. They must pay for their evil deeds to quench the fire inside my veins."

As I spoke the words, all fell silent around the hearth.

A smile formed on the erilar's lips. "It is what Attila would have said", he whispered. "And it is exactly what we will do."

Chapter 7 – Bait

"Are you sure?" Trokondas whispered.

I gestured to where twenty slaves, chained together in pairs, were labouring in the fields beyond the treeline. "I know them", I said. "They are men from Runaville."

"They could have been purchased from another village", Trokondas suggested.

"Unni overheard the men speak of their lord", I said. "They called him Oddvar."

"I suggest that we ask one of the Gautar who their lord is", Trokondas said.

"We need to catch one first", I replied, and took five solidi from my purse.

The Isaurian sighed, wearing a look of dismay. "It appears that you have spurned my teachings", he said. "Now you wish to pay the vermin."

I rubbed the gold coins together in my palm. "This is not coin", I said.

"What is it, then?" he asked.

"Bait", I replied, picked up my axe, and strolled towards the path that led from the fields to the village.

* * *

Trokondas and I watched as the exhausted slaves shuffled towards the forested path.

An armed Gautar guard led the group, with another two following at the rear of the column. Close to where we had concealed ourselves among the brambles, the lead guard raised his hand and the slaves staggered to a halt. The guard's eyes were fixed on the coin I had earlier placed on the shoulder of the path. He stepped on the gold to conceal it from the others.

"Anzo", he called out, and a younger guard trundled down the side of the column. "My woman asked me to pick some berries to add to the pottage", he said. "The meat will already be boiling above the meal-fire. She will nag at me all evening if I forget."

"I will help you", the younger guard said, but the man waved away his suggestion.

"And who will keep the slaves from darting?" the first guard asked.

Anzo conceded the point with a nod, and the column moved past. When they had disappeared around a bend in the road, the guard moved his foot and picked up the coin. For long he turned the solidus in his palm, studying the image of Leo the Thracian. It was worth ten years' wages in the lands of the savages.

Then he noticed the second coin. He glanced around in a manner displaying his suspicion, as if expecting the owner of the gold to appear at any moment. When his fears were allayed, he fell down on his hands and knees in the dirt and gently picked it up. At that moment he must have seen the glint from the edge of his vision. Another three gold coins lay in the mud.

Our quarry threw caution to the wind and charged into the mogshade, his greed getting the better of his common sense.

Trokondas grabbed the guard from behind and clamped his mouth shut in a grip of iron. The Isaurian's right arm tightened around the man's body and lifted him off the ground.

"What is the name of your lord?" I asked in the local tongue.

Trokondas relaxed his grip to allow the man to answer.

"Oddvar", he said.

"Told you so", I said, my words meant for the Isaurian.

Trokondas scowled in reply.

Thinking my friend distracted, the guard bit down on his captor's finger, drawing blood.

The big Isaurian issued a curse in the tongue of the Greeks, tightened his grip, and effortlessly snapped the man's neck as if it were a twig. He nonchalantly dropped the body onto the forest floor.

"Animal", he snarled, and spat on the corpse.

* * *

"Does the village have a wall?" Abdarakos asked.

"The boundary of the cleared area is marked by a lattice fence no higher than my shoulder", I said. "It will not even serve to keep out a hungry wolf."

The erilar issued a grunt of approval.

"But they feel secure in their numbers", I added. "We counted nearly a hundred men of fighting age. Most of the Gautar are armed with spears and flimsy shields."

"Did you glimpse the hearthmen of Oddvar?" my grandsire asked.

"We laid eyes on neither", I said. "They must have been away on a raid."

"There are two nearby villages that both owe fealty to the same lord", Trokondas said. "Ragnar and I tracked Oddvar's warriors to these villages, where they come and go as they wish. The villages are much smaller. There are no proper walls save the same lattice fence of sorts."

"How far are the villages away from the main village?" my grandsire asked.

"Five or six Roman miles", Trokondas said.

"Horses?" Abdarakos asked and took a swallow from his horn.

"They have a few", I said, "but they are used to pull carts. The Gautar do not fight from the saddle."

Again the erilar issued a grunt of approval, and a wolflike grin settled on his scarred, tattooed face. "Listen carefully", he said. "This is what we will do."

* * *

Two days later, thirty spearmen arrived from Uppsala.

The morning after, my grandsire ordered them to lay down their spears. The erilar handed us all woodcutter axes that he had purchased at the *Disting* market, and led us into the woods. None so much as issued a grumble. Even fools knew instinctively that Abdarakos was not the kind of man who tolerated defiance.

We spent ten days harvesting logs. Late afternoon each day we returned from the forest – exhausted, dirty and cold. Abdarakos did not care whether we were dead on our feet. We trained for the best part of two hours on the flat ground beside the longhouse.

When we could no longer move our limbs, we traded our swords, axes and spears for drinking horns and took our places on the furs around the large elongated hearth inside the hall, where we quenched our thirst on warm ale. While the warriors forged bonds, Runa, Unni and Atakam laboured around the meal-fire on the far side of the hall. As soon as the ale had dispelled the worst of the cold, we feasted on flatbread dipped in bowls of thick, meaty stew fortified with fresh herbs, roots and berries.

It took another ten days of toil to dig a circular trench around the great hall. We used the spoils to pack an earthen berm on the inside of the ditch. The outside wall of the berm, ten feet high, was reinforced with the logs we had harvested in the forest, while the inside sloped gently towards the hall. The timber palisade extended four feet above the top of the berm, providing us with a sheltered earthen rampart from which to repel an attack. The walkway was finished off by paving it with large blocks of turf.

Thirty-two days after felling the first tree, I stood beside Abdarakos, who was admiring our handiwork. Five of his oathsworn patrolled the rampart, which was nearly three hundred paces in length. Our large hall was situated close to the northern wall of the fort, leaving enough space to build at least another three longhouses of similar proportions.

"Do you know whose idea a circular fort was?" he asked.

I shook my head in reply.

"It was the Greek's idea", he said. "Leodis insisted that a Roman marching camp, built in a circle with a ditch and a timber-reinforced outer wall, would be strongest, easiest and quickest to build."

For long the erilar remained silent, then he sighed. "I miss Leodis", he said, turned his back to me, and walked towards the hall.

I did not follow immediately, but stared in wonder at the impressive fortifications we had built in a remarkably short time. The genius of my Greek tutor was clear to see, and it brought a smile to my face.

Abdarakos called from down the walkway, "Come, Ragnar. Let us feast this night, for tomorrow we march for the lands of Oddvar."

Chapter 8 – Oddvar

We crouched low in the undergrowth close to the fence that demarcated the perimeter of the small settlement. I held the horn bow of the khan in my fist, a three-bladed arrow nocked to the string.

Kursik motioned with his chin towards the five Gautar warriors lounging in the early morning sun outside the hall. They were whiling away the time playing a game of chance, their ale-induced exclamations altering between ones of delight and dismay, depending on the fall of the dice.

One of the men cast the bones and shouted in glee, followed by a cacophony of moans from the losers. The winner reached out, claimed his prize and stomped off, no doubt in an attempt to avoid losing whatever he had gained.

"That one is more fortunate than he realises", Kursik whispered. "He will be the messenger."

On my signal, two Hun arrows left the strings and slammed into the Gautar. Before the remaining two warriors could react, two more shafts left our bows and skewered their necks. The winner of the game of dice peered around the corner of the longhouse, and my arrow embedded in a post less than a foot from his head. He staggered backwards and disappeared from view.

Heartbeats later, chaos ensued. Townsfolk scrambled across the fence to take shelter in the woods while others rushed into their longhouses to retrieve whatever they regarded as valuable enough to be worth risking their lives for.

With the string to my ear, I studied the peasants scampering about. For a brief moment I pitied the wretches who would lose all they had before sunset.

"Let us not waste our arrows", I said, and lowered my bow.

Just then Beremud arrived, returning from his vantage point from where he had been watching the road that led to the main settlement of Oddvar. "I've owned horses that couldn't run as fast as that guard", the Goth said, and gestured with his thumb over his shoulder.

"Come, we have to get back to the erilar", I said and walked towards the three hobbled horses.

* * *

We found Abdarakos where he had cleverly concealed his warband behind a rocky outcrop overlooking Oddvar's town.

My grandsire clasped my shoulder. "We saw messengers arrive from both towns", he said. "Oddvar is a cautious one – he has sent fifteen men to each of the smaller settlements."

"Seventy warriors remain in this town", I said. "They still outnumber us two to one."

"In that you are right", Abdarakos said. "But is it not better than three to one?"

I realised the foolishness of my words, but the erilar ignored my embarrassment. "Oddvar would have heard the stories of how strange warriors had defeated his men on the beach near Runaville", he said. "But he would not have believed the words of cowards who had run from battle. He will be ready to repel an attack from the Svear, not the Heruli."

Abdarakos gave the order to advance on the settlement. Cautiously we weaved our way through the dense forest of beech and spruce. Three hundred paces from the settlement he signalled a halt, dismounted, and passed his horse's reins to a warrior.

"Come, Ragnar", he said and gestured for me to follow him. We kept to the shadows, slowly making our way in the direction of the village.

57

"I will send the thirty Svear spearmen to confront them", Abdarakos said. "The Gautar believe themselves superior to the Svear. They will attack when they see how few they are."

"And once they engage, the Huns will decimate the Gautar ranks from the flanks", I guessed. "Then the Isaurians and the Huns will crush them with a cavalry attack."

"It will work", he said, confirming my words.

Just then the erilar raised a hand, took me by the elbow, and pulled me down into a crouch behind a bilberry bush. From the hillside we had an unobstructed view of the main entrance to the village.

Oddvar had not been idle. Eighty spear-wielding warriors were milling about on the open ground inside the gate. At their centre stood a bull of a man dressed as a noble. But what drew my attention was his sixteen oathsworn warriors. All wore the arms and armour of Romans.

Abdarakos gestured to Oddvar's hearthmen. "Look at their *phalerae*", he whispered. "They are auxiliaries who fought alongside the armies of the Western Empire."

While I studied the auxiliaries, the gods opened my eyes and recognition dawned on me.

"I wish to change the plan", I said.

"Tell me then", he growled.

When I was through, my grandsire studied me intently for a while, then nodded his consent.

I stood to my full height and casually stepped into the path that led to the front gate of the settlement. I wore the armour of the elite guards of the emperor of the East. The reputation of the excubitors were known across the breadth of the Empire – even in the West.

It did not take long for the Gautar to notice me. They shouted warnings to their lord, and pointed at the warrior strolling towards them.

I came to a halt thirty paces outside the gate, drew my bearded axe from its sheath on my back, and pointed the blade at the lord of the village.

Oddvar drew his sword and led his men out the gate, coming to a halt ten paces from me.

"Finally, I lay eyes on you, Oddvar", I boomed in the local tongue. "You are a coward who makes war on the weak. Will you hide behind your men or will you dare to face a man?"

One of the hearthmen, a big man with red hair protruding from underneath his open face helmet, grabbed Oddvar's arm, restraining his lord. The auxiliary spoke at length, vigorously shaking his head. At last Oddvar relented, but jerked his arm away from the man in obvious disgust.

"What business does an excubitor have on these far shores?" the auxiliary asked in broken Latin.

I signalled with my axe, and Trokondas, Asbadus, Beremud and Kursik stepped onto the path, all resplendent in the armour of the guards of the emperor.

"My business in my own, Haldr", I growled in Latin to ensure that Oddvar would not understand my words.

The redhead staggered backwards as if he had received a blow to the chest. "How do you know my name excubitor?" he growled.

I ignored his question. "Why do you serve the Gautar, Haldr, when you are of the Svear?"

"We are Oddvar's sworn men", Haldr growled. "We were shipwrecked on these shores years ago. Oddvar captured us and gave us a choice – die, or be oathbound to him for as long as he draws breath."

"Then we have to remedy that", I said, and raised my axe above my head for the second time.

Two shafts slammed into Oddvar's chest. The armour-piercing heads split his mail and threw the corpse backwards into the ranks of his men.

"Are you with us?" I shouted to Haldr in the confusion.

Only a fool would side with rabble against four excubitors. In reply, Haldr and his sixteen companions drew their blades and turned on their masters.

"Kill them all", I boomed, and rushed to meet the enemy. From the sides of the path, the Svear spearmen, Huns and Heruli fell on the flanks of the fifty remaining Gautar.

Within ten heartbeats it was all over.

* * *

When the last of the Gautar lay dead, the Svear and Heruli surrounded Haldr and his men.

"Sheathe your blades", I commanded.

Haldr's gaze drifted between the excubitors, the Huns and Abdarakos. Wisely he slipped his reddened Roman sword into its scabbard.

I lifted my gilded helmet from my head. "Do you remember the Heruli boy you took as a slave, Haldr?" I asked, towering over the Svear.

Haldr studied me, swallowed, and licked his dry lips. Then his eyes turned wide. "You?" he stammered. "Ragnar the cripple? The one who cursed us?"

I ignored his words and placed my hand on Abdarakos's shoulder. "This is the man whom you stole me from", I said.

The erilar regarded Haldr and his men with his remaining blue-grey eye, devoid of emotion. "You fought well, Svear", he growled. "I will allow you to live. Do you wish to give an oath, or do you wish to leave? Choose before I change my mind."

"We know only the way of the sword, lord", Haldr said, and went down on one knee to give his oath.

"Not to me, fool", the erilar replied. "Is it not clear to you? Your destiny is tied with that of Ragnar's."

Haldr inclined his head and I presented the blade of my axe. One by one the sixteen Svear lay their hands on the grey iron and freely gave their oaths to Ragnar the Cripple.

Chapter 9 – Malady

The peasant townsfolk of Oddvar's village undoubtedly had no hand in the attack on Runaville months before. Their innocence mattered not – what mattered was that they were Gautar, which, in a way, made them guilty. For them it was a dark day. The ones who had been foolish enough to stay behind were unceremoniously butchered or taken as slaves.

Yet, for the many slaves from Runaville who had laboured for months under the heavy yoke of the Gautar, it was a day to give thanks to the gods. When we had freed the Svear and gathered the loot, we set the villages to the torch. I watched as the flames consumed all. For a heartbeat I thought of the teachings of Leodis, my Greek tutor, and I felt a stab of guilt, even sadness, for the fate of the Gautar. But then I purged the weakness from my heart and relished the sweet revenge. It was the way of my people after all – the way of the Sea of Grass.

* * *

Forty-eight freed Svear returned with us to Runaville. Fifteen of the thirty Gautar we had captured, Abdarakos sent east with the spearmen, as a gift to King Egil. The erilar kept all the loot.

For the first two weeks, freedman, slave and warrior toiled side by side to build the second hall which would house the original inhabitants and the newly acquired thralls.

On the evening of the day that saw the completion of the longhouse, Abdarakos hosted a feast. The townsfolk celebrated inside their new hall while the warriors feasted in theirs. My grandsire insisted that Runa and Unni continue to reside in his hall.

"One must take care", Abdarakos explained. "Never should one give the peasants the opportunity to get ideas above their station. It is what the Greeks did", he added. "And look where it got them."

With the addition of Haldr and his ex-auxiliaries, the number of our warriors had grown to thirty-four. I had told the redhead Svear my life's tale, and wide-eyed, he had declared it as the machinations of the gods.

Haldr tore into a joint of pork and swallowed it down with gulps of ale. "The Gautar will not rest", he said. "When they find out where you come from, they will strike back."

"They will think twice before they attack us again", I said. "They fear us."

The redhead glanced around the room and his gaze settled on the erilar. "I heard that he once led the armies of the great khan", he mused.

"He did", I confirmed. "And the man beside him was the champion of the Huns."

"The Gautar doesn't know that", Haldr said, and leaned in closer as if he wished to impart a secret. "Oddvar was kin of the king of the Gautar", he said. "They will come."

Later that evening I informed Abdarakos of the words of Haldr.

"Kin of the Gautar king", he growled. "It changes nothing. When they come, we will kill them." He drank deeply from his ale horn. "Or, if it is our fate, they will kill us."

The following morning, life in the village returned to normal for the first time in many moons. The farmers started toiling in the fields and the fishermen set out to sea. Children took goats and cows to pasture while their mothers brewed ale or made cheese.

The warriors, under the guidance of Abdarakos, spent their time training with sword, bow and spear, or laboured to improve the defences of the village. While Haldr and the Heruli deepened the ditch around the wall, Trokondas, Asbadus, Kursik, Beremud and I wielded axes to clear the trees around the village. Soon the sinews in our shoulders, backs and arms were thick and hard as the oaks we felled.

The little free time I had, I spent in the company of Unni. I was certain that I wanted her as my woman, yet it was as if the gods robbed me of my ability to use my tongue each time I wished to ask her.

I broached the subject with Runa.

"Yes", the old woman confirmed, her eyes narrow. "I know of it. It is an ailment, a sickness."

"Can it be cured?" I asked, suddenly concerned.

"Three nights from today there will be a full moon", she said, and handed me a small leather sachet filled with black powder. "Mix this into a large cup of mead before you go to her. Speak with her under the light of the full moon and the bonds that bind your tongue will fall away."

Late afternoon three days later, while training with the warriors I sheathed my axe. "I need to take a potion to heal an ailment", I said.

My friends said naught but regarded me with concern.

"The seer said that I will be cured by the potion", I said, putting their minds at rest.

I walked down to the stream and washed the grime from my body. At the hall I combed my beard and hair and dressed in a clean tunic. I poured myself a large cup of mead, mixed in the powder, and swallowed the strong, golden liquid down with one, long gulp.

Atakam sat beside the hearth grinding up herbs with a mortar and pestle. "Runa gave you a potion?" he asked.

I shared the story with him.

"I concur with Runa", he said. "She is wise indeed."

Already feeling the effects of the potion, I set off to locate Unni. I found her at the back of the hall in the stables, tending to a newborn goat.

When she was done, I took her by the hand. We strolled down the path that led to the beach where we made ourselves comfortable on a large rock overlooking the bay. Soon, a bright yellow moon rose above the dark water. The time had come to break the bonds and speak the words.

"Unni", I said, "I wish to speak with you."

"What do you wish to tell me, Ragnar?" she said and moved closer to me.

I pressed an open palm against her warm cheek and silently thanked the gods for unchaining my tongue.

"Ragnar", Unni said again, this time with more urgency. "Ragnar, look", she said and pointed to where Mani illuminated the Austmarr.

The keels of seven large longships sliced the mirror surface of the water, silently gliding towards the shingle beach.

* * *

Abdarakos did not bother to ask me if I knew who the boats belonged to – it would have been a question befitting a fool.

While we strapped on our armour and blades, my grandsire issued the orders. "They believe that they will catch us unawares", he said. "We will wait for them in the dark woods and cut off the head of the serpent. Seven boats carry more than two hundred warriors - too many for us kill." He gestured to the Huns. "Sigizan, you and three men with horn bows will cover our retreat. Haldr, guard the gate and make sure you open it for us and not for the Gautar", he jested and slapped the Svear on the back.

The thick oak doors creaked closed behind us. Two of the Huns positioned themselves on each side of the path leading up to the gate. They lay down flat to conceal themselves, their bows strung and ready.

Abdarakos led the remaining fourteen warriors into the woods. Fifty paces down the path he ordered a halt and signalled for Trokondas, Beremud, Asbadus, Kursik, Boarex and me to join him on the slope above the trail. The others melted into the darkness on the opposite side of the track.

We had hardly concealed ourselves when we heard the telltale signs of many men approaching along the winding path.

A hundred heartbeats later the first of the Gautar skulked past our hiding place. Abdarakos allowed fifteen, maybe twenty men to pass before he burst from the darkness, his blade flashing like a scythe.

A helmeted warrior half-turned to face me, his eyes wide and fearful. My axe was already on its path and his head disappeared in a spray of red. I drove my armour-clad shoulder into the man beside him, who was trying to bring his sword to bear. My axe struck low and he crumpled to the ground.

"Retreat", Abdarakos boomed. I turned towards the fort and, joining the others, ran back as fast as I could. Behind me I heard the shouts of the Gautar as they came to grips with the happenings.

The Gautar were fast. Unencumbered by armour, they closed the gap. The first Hun arrows sliced through the darkness and slammed into the Gautar leading the chase. Again and again a wave of shafts left the powerful horn, wood and sinew bows, halting the Gautar charge.

Although my blood was up, relief flooded over me as soon as the last of us entered the fort and Haldr and his men lifted the locking bars into their brackets.

"Where is the erilar?" I heard Sigizan ask, and by the tone of his voice, I already knew the answer.

Chapter 10 – Tree (May 472 AD)

The enemy did not attack the fort that night, in fact there was no sign of them. But with the arrival of first light, we noticed movement within the woods.

"They will show him to us soon", Sigizan said. "Dead or alive."

The thought of what Abdarakos would be forced to endure while in the clutches of the Gautar made me wish to rush to the woods, blade in hand. I met Sigizan's eyes and it was clear that the Hun shared my sentiment.

I became aware of a commotion behind me – Unni was helping Atakam up the slope towards the rampart.

"It is the will of the gods", Atakam declared when he stood beside us.

"We will free him, or die trying", Sigizan growled. "We will attack as soon as it is dark."

"No", the shaman said, and turned to leave.

Sigizan issued a curse in defiance.

Atakam stopped in his tracks, glanced over his shoulder, and said, "You will attack when the gods will it."

"Tell us when", the Hun growled.

"I cannot", Atakam replied.

"Why not?" Sigizan asked.

"Because the gods haven't told me yet", the old shaman said, and sat down on the turf of the rampart above the gate. He closed his eyes and started to chant in the language of the ancients while he knotted linden bark between his fingers to aid him in his dreamwork.

All knew that he was travelling up the world tree to the realm of the gods. None dared to disturb or gainsay him.

* * *

When the sun was low in the sky, Atakam was yet to return from the land of the gods, and there was still no sign of Abdarakos.

Suddenly the shaman shuddered as if in the throes of a fit, fell onto his side, and opened his eyes. Although the day had turned cold, the old man was drenched in sweat. I had been raised by Atakam and held no fear of the shaman. I rushed to him and helped him gain his feet, allowing him to lean against the wood with his back to the distant trees. He drank from the wineskin I held to his lips and nodded his thanks.

Without turning his head, Atakam said, "Look towards the woods."

All turned their gaze to the treeline where a group of Gautar warriors emerged from the mogshade. They half-dragged, half-carried a blood-smeared body. Sigizan and the Huns had arrows to the strings of their bows in less than a heartbeat.

"Fools", the shaman hissed, staying their hands.

Two Gautar supported the old warrior against the trunk of an ancient ash. A third raised the erilar's hands above his head. My grandsire must have resisted, as a fourth warrior struck him in the face.

"He lives", Sigizan growled and drew the string to his ear, no doubt ready to skewer the culprit.

"The time is not right", the shaman hissed and lowered the bow with his hand.

Sigizan relented reluctantly.

"When is the time right?" the Hun growled.

"When the eastern sky turns orange", Atakam replied and gestured for me to help him down the rampart to the hall.

I assisted the shaman down the slope while in the distance I heard the thuds of the Gautar nailing Abdarakos's palms to the trunk of the ash.

* * *

Sigizan gestured at the erilar, his hand trembling with anger. "I will heed the gods", he sneered, "so we will attack at daybreak, when the eastern horizon is aflame."

I knew by then that Atakam spoke in riddles. Is it not the way of seers and shamans?

"Is that what he means, Sigi?" I asked.

"What else?" he replied.

I had no answer to the Hun's question so I kept my counsel. We stood in silence atop the rampart, watching the sun set, knowing that the odds of thirty-three men against two hundred were almost insurmountable.

The sun was still visible when a Gautar warrior, flanked by his hearthmen, approached the walls of the fort. They came to a halt forty paces from the rampart.

"I am Prince Herebeald, son of Hrethel, king of the Gautar", the man boomed proudly. I gave his words to my fellow warriors.

"I have been told that you are warriors of renown from the lands of the East", he said. "If you lay down your weapons and surrender the village to me, I will accept your oaths. The Gautar have made peace with the Danes. It is only a matter of time before we drive the Svear into the Austmarr."

He paused for effect and continued. "Defy me, and tomorrow at dawn I will slit the old man's throat" he said and gestured to Abdarakos.

As Herebeald turned around, the erilar mustered all his remaining strength. "Kill them all", he shouted, but it came out as a nearly inaudible croak.

Immediately he was silenced by the fist of a Gautar, leaving my grandsire's head hanging limply to the side. I prayed to the gods that he would live until the morning.

* * *

We did not discuss the offer made by the Gautar prince. None raised the issue – to do so would have been dishonourable.

But there were men amongst us not bound by ties of blood or oaths – my mentor Trokondas, and Asbadus the Isaurian. I found them at the far side of the rampart, staring at the faraway beach where the ships of the Gautar were still visible in the fading light.

Patiently they listened to my words.

"We do not need an oath to die for Abdarakos", Trokondas replied. "He would have done the same for us."

Asbadus grunted his agreement, not taking his eyes off the whetstone that he was running along the grey Seric iron blade of his bearded axe.

I turned to leave, but noticed a flickering light from the corner of my eye. Orange-yellow flames erupted from the Gautar ships grounded on the faraway beach. Like apparitions from another realm, four enormous longships glided onto the shingles fifty paces upwind of the burning vessels. Warriors streamed over the sides, their scale and chain glinting in the firelight.

Mourdagos, great lord of the Boat Heruli, had returned to the lands of the Svear.

* * *

The Gautar had never before faced the terror of the Steppes.

Haldr and his men had hardly pushed open the gate when the first arrows struck the guards surrounding the erilar. Riding beside Sigizan, I drew the string of Attila's bow to my ear. I held my breath and waited for the moment in time when all four hooves were free of the ground. Aided by the speed of my mount, the arrow struck like the hammer of a god, cleaving the skull of a Gautar about to spear Abdarakos.

The Huns' arrows poured into the enemy surrounding the erilar. Their well-aimed shafts kept the Gautar from opening his throat.

In less than ten heartbeats we were upon them. I slipped my bow into its case and gripped the haft of my axe near the butt for maximum reach. Trokondas, Asbadus and Beremud mirrored my actions.

We slammed into the Gautar who were spilling from the shadows in an attempt to reach Abdarakos. I swung from high, split a skull, and noticed a warrior lunging from the rear. I wheeled around but only felt the spray of blood as Trokondas's axe took the assailant's arm before he disappeared underneath the hooves. Another Gautar took advantage of the distraction, running at me with a spear aimed at my horse's belly. A Hun lasso snaked from Kursik's hand and snapped back the man's neck, yanking him from his feet.

A primal roar erupted from among the trees as Mourdagos and his warriors flooded into the enemy camp. The Gautar no longer attempted to reach Abdarakos - they scampered through the woods like a herd of deer desperate to get away from a pack of bloodthirsty wolves.

Chapter 11 – Verina

Abdarakos lay flat on his back on a straw-stuffed mattress not far from the hearth. I held my hand above his mouth to convince myself that he still drew breath, as his bare, battle-scarred chest barely moved.

Runa held the old warrior's hand. "He wanders the place of shadows between the world of men and the realm of the gods", she said. "He is struggling to find his way back to us. Some never do."

On the other side of the bed Atakam sat cross-legged with his eyes closed, no doubt travelling the spirit world in search of the erilar.

Mourdagos, the war leader of the Boat Heruli, put his arm around my shoulders and led me outside.

"He is strong, Ragnar", the big man growled. "Soon he will recover, then we will celebrate the defeat of the Gautar. Command the women to brew ale because when Abdarakos wakes, he will be thirsty."

Mourdagos had returned as he had promised. But more than that, he had brought with him fifty-three young warriors who did not wish to live under the rule of the new king. Rodolph was leading the Heruli on a path that diverged from the way of the warrior. It was a path which not all wished to tread.

The big man leaned forward, gripping the wooden balustrade outside the hall in his bearlike paws. He gestured with his bearded chin to the men toiling to build another longhouse. "All these men wish to keep the old ways alive", he said. "They have hardly arrived in the lands of the Svear and already they are content having reddened their blades and filled their chests with loot."

"Rodolph advocates peace", Mourdagos growled. "Every time I hear the word, I feel the yellow bile rise in my throat."

"Peace!" he spat. "What is peace but an excuse for sloth and cowardice? The Heruli will have peace when our enemies tremble in fear at the mention of our name. Only fear brings lasting peace – all else is but an illusion."

"The Gautar have witnessed the power of the Heruli", the boat lord said. "But it will take time before they fear you." He lowered his voice and glanced around to make sure none were listening. "The Svear will have to learn to fear you as well."

Before I could offer a reply, Unni arrived. "You are needed inside", she said.

81

When she was out of earshot, Mourdagos said, "You need to make her your woman, Ragnar, or someone else will take her." With that he turned his back to me and led the way into the hall.

We found my grandfather breathing heavily, his eyes open wide. "Nine days", Mourdagos said and gently placed a hand on Abdarakos's arm. "You wandered the other side for nine days."

"I have seen many things", Abdarakos said.

"Tell us", Mourdagos replied, eager to hear the words of a man who had taken a peek through the veil separating the worlds.

"I will, brother", my grandsire said. "But first I thirst for ale."

* * *

More than a moon passed before Abdarakos was his old self again. Mourdagos had insisted on delaying the victory celebrations until his brother-in-law was fit to lead it.

Mourdagos, Trokondas and Kursik accompanied me on a hunt to find wild boar and deer for the feast table.

The domain of the Boat Heruli bordered the Amber Road, which not only served as a conduit for trade, but also for gossip. We had had little news of the happenings in the lands of Rome.

"Any news from the Empire?" Trokondas asked, riding abreast of Mourdagos.

The lord of the Boat Heruli shook his head. "A Roman merchant told me that the year started with a dark omen. Vulcan, the terrible god of fire, shook the earth and hurled molten rock into the heavens. For weeks on end thick clouds of ash obscured the sun. In Rome, the people's heads were covered with ash whenever they dared to venture outside."

Trokondas nodded in grim agreement.

"Not long after the ominous sign, the peace talks between Ricimer, the lord high general of the West, and Anthemius, the Western Emperor, failed", he said. "Last I heard, Ricimer was marching on Rome to confront the emperor."

"Any news of Prince Ottoghar?" I asked.

"He has remained loyal to Ricimer and his warband is part of the high general's army", Mourdagos explained.

"I trust that things are better in the East?" Trokondas asked.

"Barely", Mourdagos continued. "The Thracian Goths revolted after Aspar was killed. Word is that Leo has sent Zeno and Basiliscus, his wife's brother, to quell the revolt."

"Yes, Leo the Thracian is still holding on to power", Mourdagos said, answering our unasked question, "even though he is frail and sickly. Rumour has it that he will soon appoint his grandson, the son of Zeno and his daughter Ariadne, as Caesar."

"I know that your brother, Illus, has sent for you, Trokondas", Mourdagos continued. "When I return to my lands you are welcome to join the voyage south, should you wish."

"I prefer life among the Svear", Trokondas replied. "Here, it is easy to know who the enemy is. In the City of Constantine friends and enemies are difficult to distinguish from one another. Sometimes a friend in the morning becomes an enemy at sunset."

Kursik, who led our group, signalled caution with a raised hand. "Sometimes a boar which roams the forest in the morning is destined to become a meal in the evening", he jested and pointed to tracks at the side of the path.

We dismounted, tied the horses to a tree, and entered the thicket with our boar spears at the ready. Kursik, whose senses rivalled that of the forest dwelling creatures, led the way.

When we had advanced three or four hundred paces, the Hun went to a crouch. Kursik pushed aside a curtain of ferns and pointed to a clearing where a few large male boars were digging in the forest floor, feeding on roots and grubs.

We selected two animals, rose from our hiding place, and cast our heavy spears, which all found their marks. As we emerged into the clearing to claim our prizes, a piercing screech split the silence of the forest. A monster of a boar, as old as the mountains, stormed from the undergrowth. The huge male's scarred coat was as black as night, with a mane streaked with grey. Its ears resembled the leaves of an oak, ripped apart in countless struggles with bears and wolves. One yellow tusk was nearly as long as my forearms, the other was not much more than a stub – no doubt broken in a death duel many years before.

The hog's deep-set, beady eyes were focused on Trokondas who was yet to arm himself. By the will of the gods my bearded weapon was already in my fist. I drew back the axe and cast it at the boar with all my might. The weapon whistled through the air and the blade struck true. It embedded in the beast's forehead, the razor-sharp iron cleaving its skull. The boar's forelegs collapsed and it ploughed into the leaf carpet at Trokondas's feet.

For long, none spoke, until Kursik broke the silence. He circled the carcass of the boar, which must have weighed more than three men. "I hope you are hungry", he said, unclipped a wineskin from his belt, and took a swallow before passing it to Trokondas.

* * *

That night at the feast, all were in good spirits, except Trokondas, who only sipped on his ale.

We told tales of bravery, reliving the battle against the Gautar.

Mourdagos told of how I had slain the beast roasting over the coals. "Four men could not carry it, so we left it where it died and brought its piglet instead", he jested, and pointed at the carcass of the massive boar.

Once all had told their ale-induced stories and we could laugh and cheer no more, I went to find my mentor. He sat beside Asbadus, who had succumbed to the effects of the food and ale, and was lying on his arms on the table, snoring loudly.

"You saved my life", Trokondas said and gestured for me to take a seat opposite him.

"And you gave me the skills to do it", I replied as I collapsed onto the bench. "So, it makes us even."

The hulking Isaurian ignored my words. "I wish to tell you something", he said, a serious expression settling on his face. "It is a secret that you must take to the grave."

He placed his blade on the tabletop. "Swear it", he said.

I waved away his words. "You know I will never tell", I said.

Trokondas thumped the table with an open palm. "Swear it, Ragnar", he growled. "Swear it on your mother's grave."

I realised then that it was no time for jests, and I did as he asked.

"I came close to death today", he said. "Some secrets need to be shared before one crosses the Styx."

"Emperor Leo founded the excubitors in the year 461. It was a year filled with turmoil. Leo became his own man and refused to bend to the will of Aspar. The emperor spent many days garnering the support he needed to ensure the continuation of his rule. I spent long days and nights guarding his wife, Verina, and their two daughters."

Trokondas wetted his throat with ale and continued. "She was a very, very beautiful woman", he said. "A lonely, beautiful woman with a husband that was never there."

He grinned and said, "It is not what you think, Ragnar."

"Verina became pregnant with her third child and nine months later she brought a healthy boy into the world. He was the only boychild, the heir to the throne. Weeks after the birth the boy became ill with a malady that none of the physicians could cure."

"I was the one who caught the wetnurse poisoning the babe. She fed him a little bit of the powder every day, to make it look like an ailment. It did not take much to make her spill the beans. Aspar had paid her to murder the child. There was no use in dragging the untouchable high general before the courts. He was the most powerful man in the Empire, above the law in every way."

Trokondas hung his head in shame. "She pleaded with me to lie for her", he said. "But I needed little convincing. I found her a child's corpse – one of the hundreds that perish daily in the greatest city on earth."

He took a long swallow from his ale horn. "Everyone expected the emperor's sickly child to die, so none raised an eyebrow when Verina announced the lie. Not even Leo, who was too busy defending his throne against Aspar. The empress asked Zeno to deliver the news of the child's demise to her kin in Thrace. She ordered him to send me, as she trusted me implicitly."

I took the cloth-wrapped babe and rode from the city. My men waved me through without so much as a second glance. They would never have dared to delay me, never mind search me. Verina's gold bought the services of a wetnurse in the closest town. Together we made our way west, towards Dardania in the prefecture of Illyricum. We eventually found the little hamlet called Baderiana and delivered the babe into the hands of an old woman - the same peasant woman who used to be the wetnurse of Verina many years before. She wept when I gave her the pouch of gold and read her the message from her empress. The old woman gave me her oath that she would look after the child. Verina left just one request – that the boy would be named Justin, after her grandfather."

"Before I fled the long reach of Aspar, she made me promise that one day I would search for the boy and take him into the ranks of the excubitors. She wished for him to be a warrior, not a swine-herding peasant all his life."

"If I perish, there is none to honour the oath", he said. "That is the reason why the empress rescued you from the clutches of Zeno. It was not about you, but me. And, also, she hated Aspar with all her being."

Again, he extended his blade. "Promise me that you will find the boy if I die before I honour my oath."

I laid my hand on the iron and did as he wished.

Chapter 12 – Tonne (July 472 AD)

The Great City of Constantine was many thousands of miles from Runaville, and even further from my thoughts. Although my oath had given peace to Trokondas, soon it was but a memory banished to a far corner of my mind.

Mourdagos and his men were preparing their boats for the return journey. He had decided that the Boat Heruli would travel south, raiding the Gautar settlements along the coast.

Abdarakos had purchased a longship from the boat lord. This meant that he owned two boats, as one of the smaller Gautar ships had emerged from the fire unscathed and the erilar had laid claim to it.

While we loaded amphorae filled with ale and water onto the ships, a messenger arrived at the hall of Abdarakos. Although most of the Heruli had mastered the basics of the Svear language by then, my grandsire was not fool enough to make decisions based on a partial understanding.

Haldr, who had been guarding the fort, came to summon me.

"The old man has called for you", he said in the tongue of the Svear.

"Be careful what you say about Abdarakos", I said. "He has had men flayed alive for lesser transgressions."

I noticed Haldr glance around, suddenly concerned about who had heard and understood his words.

I walked with him. "I will say that you spoke of the shaman", I said, laying his fears to rest. "The worst he can do is doom your shade for all eternity."

I left a scowling Haldr at the gate of the fort and made my way to the hall, where I found Abdarakos and Trokondas in discussion. A man, presumably the messenger, was standing awkwardly at the side of the hall.

The erilar issued a grunt and waved his hand, a clear gesture for the messenger to approach.

"My lords", the man said, and cleared his throat. "King Egil has requested that you come to his assistance. A bondsman of his, a freed thrall, has revolted and is causing mischief in his lands. He requests the help of you and your warriors, lords. Of course, you will be well rewarded."

I gave my grandsire his words.

"How does a freedman manage to cause so much mischief?" Abdarakos asked.

I translated his words.

"The king gave no such message", the Svear said.

Abdarakos slowly came to his feet, his hand on the hilt of his sword. He advanced on the messenger and came to a halt a pace away. "I am asking you, not the king", he said.

The messenger swallowed, no doubt weighing up his options. He wisely decided that he would rather face the wrath of the Svear king than that of the erilar.

"Lord", he said and inclined his head. "King Egil gave Tonne, a former thrall, control over his gold."

"Peasants and thralls are not to be trusted", Trokondas growled. "What fool gives his gold to a freedman?"

"How many men does this freedman have?" Trokondas asked.

"More than the king", the messenger blurted out, having thrown caution to the wind.

"He asked you how many", Abdarakos growled.

"Two, maybe three hundred", he said.

My grandsire reached into his purse and flipped a silver coin to the messenger who adroitly snatched it from the air. "Tell your king that we will come", he said and dismissed the man with a wave of his hand.

* * *

Accompanied by Mourdagos, our five ships glided into Mälaren Bay where we soon overhauled a local fisherman who had feverishly tried to outrow us. In return for a few silvers, he guided us through the vast network of channels of the lake until, three days later, our hulls grinded to a stop on the shingle beach two miles south of Uppsala.

Unni and Runa, who had accompanied us on the trip as healers, remained on board with a handful of warriors.

King Egil, who had been alerted to our arrival, met us off the beach.

He openly gaped at the hundred and fifty heavily armed and armoured men disembarking from the longships. Mourdagos had brought a further six horses from the southern lands, increasing our mounted contingent to twelve.

Of course, the king had no way of knowing that our numbers had grown fivefold. He clearly displayed his vacillating emotions on his face. His initial expression of pleasure faded and was replaced by one of concern, as he no doubt realised that there would be only one outcome should we decide to turn on him.

Abdarakos reined in ten paces from the Svear ruler and inclined his head, but did not dismount. In the brutal world of the Heruli, respect followed reputation, which could not be acquired by titles, but had to be earned. "Lord king", the erilar said. "We came at your request."

"I am pleased that your numbers have been bolstered", Egil replied. "Come, join me in my hall. My men will show your warriors where to make camp."

When Gautar slaves had filled our horns with foaming ale, the king briefed us. "I have known Tonne from boyhood", he said. "He was the son of a slave, a fosterling in the court of my father, Aun. Although he is but a thrall, he is resourceful."

"My father freed him many years ago and made him responsible for the gold of the kingdom. Tonne is a shrewd man – the growing hoard of gold is a testament to his worth."

The king wetted his throat and continued. "But he became arrogant, so I decided to re-enslave him due to his lack of gratitude."

"What did the thrall do?" Abdarakos asked.

"He married", the king sneered, "without asking for my permission. What arrogance! I had him taken during the night and clapped in chains. But he is a conniving man who has used my gold to recruit warriors to his cause. That same evening his men set him free, killing a handful of my hearthmen in the process."

"Have you tried to recapture him since?" the erilar asked.

"Our forces have clashed", Egil said. "But they were minor skirmishes."

"How many times?" Abdarakos asked.

"Eight", Egil said and averted his gaze in shame.

"And the thrall defeated you every time?" Abdarakos asked, a slight frown on his brow.

"Tonne is a servant of the dark gods", Egil countered. "And as slippery and dangerous as a serpent. He is encamped but ten miles to the north. Like a vulture he is waiting to feast upon our corpses."

That evening we drank sparingly and retired early.

On the morrow we rose before dawn. When we had strapped on our armour, we meticulously checked our gear and weapons. I inspected the haft of my axe for the telltale signs of cracks while

Kursik repeatedly drew his horn bow, then ran his fingers along the sinew string. Trokondas gently slid a whetstone along the edge of the head of his axe, tested the keenness with his finger, and wiped it with an oiled rag. He issued a grunt of approval and secured it in its leather sheath. A damaged weapon, blunt blade or loose strap could easily mean the difference between life and death.

Abdarakos, flanked by Mourdagos, led the Heruli from the camp.

King Egil, mounted on what looked like a plough horse, waited for us at the head of his army of two hundred men.

Abdarakos stared at the assembled Svear, sizing up their quality.

"The snake has whittled us down bit by bit", Egil said. "We have but half the number we had months before."

Excuses did not sit well with the erilar. He ignored the words of the king. "Tonne will not know of the presence of the Heruli army", he growled. "You must advance against him. My men will shadow you and we will fall upon the enemy when you are engaged in battle."

We trailed the army of the Svear by at least a mile. I rode beside Abdarakos and Mourdagos.

"It seems like Tonne is a more capable king than Egil",
Mourdagos mused. "Were it not that he had been a slave, we
could have supported him, rather than Egil."

"I agree", Abdarakos said. "Once a thrall, always a thrall. They
have no honour."

"It will not do to destroy the slave's army", I said. "Egil will
need the men to fight alongside him in future. Tonne and the
traitorous lords will have to die, but the lives of his men must be
spared."

"It is easier said than done", my grandsire said.

"Allow me to try", I said.

Abdarakos grunted his approval and I could not help but notice
pride in his eyes.

* * *

Kursik and Boarex rode at my side, with Trokondas, Asbadus and
Beremud following close behind.

The Huns reined in close to the treeline. "There", Kursik
whispered and used his strung bow to point at the army of the

97

thrall, arrayed to our right. His spearmen were drawn up in orderly ranks, all issued with shields of similar design. At the centre of their line, in the front rank, was a man dressed as a noble. He wore an open face iron helmet and Roman mail.

To our left, the warriors of Egil were advancing. Compared to Tonne's men they appeared to be a disorganised mob. Egil also rode at the centre, but at the rear of the ranks, screened by his hearthmen.

The two armies engaged with a clash of blades. We waited patiently, watching as events unfolded.

At first it seemed as if the two opposing forces were evenly matched. All of a sudden, the tide turned in the favour of Tonne. Egil's men were pushed back and they glanced over their shoulders looking to the king for guidance.

To my surprise Egil did not flee, but spurred his mount forward to engage Tonne's men. His actions served to bolster the resolve of his hearthmen as they, too, surged forward to protect their king. But then a spear struck the king in his side and he fell from the saddle.

An almighty sigh could be heard from the lines of the king's army. A brave oathsworn mounted Egil's horse and draped the injured king across its neck. He jerked the horse's head to the rear and galloped away to take his lord to safety.

Thinking the battle lost and the king mortally wounded, his warriors cast down their weapons and ran. For the first time that day, Tonne's men broke rank and stormed after the fleeing enemy, throwing all caution to the wind.

"Now", I said and dug my heels into the sides of my warhorse. The powerful animal powered to a gallop within a few strides. Convinced that victory was theirs, Tonne's men were committed to the chase, and few noticed the new threat. Hun arrows skewered the necks of the men who turned to face us.

Thirty paces from our prey, a hearthman alerted Tonne to the danger. He shouted commands and his oathsworn tried to rally to protect their lord. As arranged, Trokondas, Asbadus and I moved to the front, our long-hafted bearded axes in our fists. I swung down heavily, my axe splitting the shield of a hearthman before my mount's shoulder spun him to the side. I saw Trokondas rise with the aid of his stirrups. He leaned over to his left, swept his blade backhanded, and two men crumpled to the ground. I felt a spear strike my lower back, but it failed to pierce the heavy scales and mail. I turned to deal with the threat, only to see Boarex's lasso snake around my attacker's neck.

To Tonne's credit – he stood his ground. The blade of my axe split his raised shield and struck his helmet, sending him to the land of the gods.

Moments later, a ramshorn announced the arrival of Abdarakos. Armour-clad Heruli warriors emerged from the treeline, their scale and chain reflecting the morning sun.

Silence descended upon the field of battle.

"Your lord is dead", I boomed. "Give your oath to King Egil, and he will spare you if he lives. Do not redden your blades with the blood of your kin. Keep your weapons sharp for when the Gautar come to take your wives and children as their slaves."

My words were meant for the ears of Tonne's men. In the realm of the sky, the gods were listening. But listening was not all that they did - they were laughing as well.

Chapter 13 – Wound

Unni gently held Egil in a seated position to ensure that he would not choke.

"He has to live", Runa said, and scooped another spoonful of boiled leeks from the copper pot into the delirious king's mouth.

"I did not know that leeks cured a stomach wound", I heard Kursik mutter.

"It doesn't, Hun", Runa croaked and fixed him with a sidelong glance.

Kursik, who had been watching the woman treat the wound, muttered something incomprehensible and joined Boarex at the far side of the hall.

Unni laid Egil down, then handed the seer a pot of boiling water. Runa immersed a linen rag into the hot liquid. Thirty heartbeats later she lifted the steaming cloth from the water. Meticulously she wiped the blood from the finger-long cut in the king's side. Then Runa closed her eyes and chanted a mantra only her kind could understand. For the best part of an hour, she sat at the king's bedside. Suddenly she stopped chanting and leaned over, her face inches from the wound. She pulled the deep wound open and sniffed.

"He will live", Runa proclaimed for all to hear.

"Did the gods tell her?" I asked Atakam who sat beside me.

"No", the shaman replied.

"The smell of leeks was absent", he said. "The iron of the spear did not pierce his intestines."

When the medicine woman had bound the king's wound, I approached her. "Why is it so important to you that he lives?" I asked.

Her eyes narrowed and a slight smile played around the corners of her mouth. "It is not", she replied. "I care little whether he lives or dies", she said.

In response a frown furrowed my brow.

"The only thing I care about is the manner of his death", she hissed, turned away from me, and shuffled towards the meal-fire.

* * *

The Heruli kept the peace while Runa and Unni nursed the king.

Two weeks after Tonne's death, the wound had knitted together and the king could walk unassisted.

Egil announced that, three days hence, a great feast would be held at Uppsala to honour the gods for delivering the thrall into his hands. Abdarakos and Mourdagos, impatient as they were, agreed to stay until the day after the celebrations.

In preparation for the big day, loads of wood were carted from the forest, animals were slaughtered and ale purchased from the surrounding villages. On the afternoon of the feast day, on the flat ground facing the great hall, pigs, oxen and sheep were spitted above roaring hardwood fires. Ale and mead flowed freely and when dusk arrived, the sounds of laughter and song dominated the feasting ground.

Before the ale completely dulled the senses of the men, King Egil appeared at the top of the wooden steps outside the hall. He raised his hands, requesting silence. Patiently the king waited for the cheering to subside.

"Tonight, we feast to give thanks to the gods", he said. "In their great wisdom they have chosen me above Tonne the thrall to govern the lands of the Svear."

His words solicited a round of cheers.

"But", he said, "I am yet to pass judgement on the warriors who fought on the side of the usurper."

Five Svear lords who had supported Tonne stepped from the hall and kneeled in front of their king, their heads inclined in supplication.

Egil drew his blade and stepped forward. One by one the Svear lords lay their sword hands upon the iron and swore fealty to him. He raised them by their hands and placed a silver torque around each lord's neck, thereby binding them to him until death. They were now his sworn followers, his ringmen.

The king embraced each lord, who, followed by their warriors, joined the feast.

But the king was not through.

When the raucous had died down, he continued. "It is high time that I take a bride", he said. "To ensure that the royal line remains unbroken."

All assembled shouted their agreement with the words of the king - even I joined in. I felt eyes on me and stole a glance to the side. Atakam was watching me intently, causing a chill to run down my spine.

The king signalled with his hand and from the doors of the hall, Unni appeared. I experienced a sensation akin to cold iron piercing my chest and cleaving my heart. Involuntarily the ale horn dropped from my fist and I staggered backwards.

104

A strong arm clamped around my shoulders, steadying me.

"Ulgin can be fickle", Mourdagos whispered. "Do not swim against the current, Ragnar."

Despite his words I decided that, this time, I would defy the gods.

* * *

Ignoring the stares of my friends, I left in search of the old seer. I found Runa in her tent, reclining on the furs with her back to the open flap.

"Come in, Ragnar", she sighed.

I did as she asked and joined her on the floor.

"Not all wounds are inflicted by a blade", she said, and poured us each a cup of mead.

"Why?" I asked, the desperation thick in my voice.

To my annoyance the old crone burst out laughing and doubled over, spilling mead on the furs.

"'Why', you ask" she said when she had regained her composure, and drank what remained in her cup. "The answer is always the same, boy", she said. "It is because the gods will it so, you fool."

105

"I will go to her", I said. "I will ask her to deny Egil and become my wife."

Again, the old crone doubled over with laughter. "And you think you can defy the will of the gods?" she asked.

"I do not think so, woman", I said, feeling the anger rise like black bile. "I know so."

I stood to leave, but she grabbed my wrist. Surprised at the strength of her bony claw, I paused for a heartbeat.

"Swim with the current, Ragnar" she said, "not against it", and released my hand.

When I arrived at the great hall, the feast was in full swing. King Egil walked amongst his warriors, sharing their tales and jests. Of Unni there was no sign.

Atakam must have noticed me standing on the fringes, and slowly made his way towards me.

"You search for the bride of Egil?" he asked.

Atakam did not wait for an answer, but pointed at a small hall, furthest from the feast. "She has retired for the night. She sleeps where it is safe – inside the hall where the king keeps his gold."

I grunted my thanks, turned, and strode towards the distant longhouse. The shaman let me be.

106

I found Unni outside the hall. She was leaning on the wooden hitching rail, staring into the darkness.

"You came!" she shouted and ran to me.

I caught her in an embrace and held her for long. "I have tried to ask you so many times, that I have lost count of the number", I said. "Now it is too late", I added and felt as if my shade slipped into a dark abyss.

"The king has asked me for my hand in marriage", Unni said. "That much is true. But I have not given him an answer yet."

"But the king said…", I started.

She withdrew from the embrace. "He assumes every woman dream of becoming a queen", she replied.

"Do you?" I asked.

Unni offered no reply and I realised that I would be digging my own grave if I continued my line of questioning, so I did what was long overdue.

"Will you marry me?" I asked.

Unni leaned in close and kissed me on the cheek. "You will have to wait and see", she said. "I do not know whether I would prefer to be the wife of Ragnar the Cripple or the queen of all the Svear."

She smiled sweetly, turned her back to me, and entered the heavily guarded hall, leaving me standing in the darkness like the fool I was.

I skulked back the way I had come, berating myself for thinking that I could challenge the will of the gods. Only two hours had passed since Egil's words had plunged my shade into darkness. Now my heart soared again.

I walked as if in a trance, preoccupied with the happenings, unaware of my surroundings. The sounds of warriors feasting drowned out the sounds of the night.

Just then I noticed a group of Svear warriors running towards me, shouting and pointing in my direction. My hand found the hilt of my axe, but before I drew the blade, I realised that their ire was not directed at me, but at something behind me.

I swung around to find the night sky bathed in an orange hue. The treasure hall of Egil was aflame.

Chapter 14 – Treasure

Scattered around the burning hall lay the bloodied corpses of eight of Egil's hearthmen. The attackers had carried off their own dead, leaving no trace of whence they had come.

While the Svear stared at the spectacle, I jogged towards the greenwood, heading for the forested path that led to the shingle beach.

One of Mourdagos's longships had been taken. The other four, silhouetted against the night sky in the channel, had managed to evade the raiders. Four greybeards, warriors whom Mourdagos had left on board to guard the boat, floated facedown in the shallows close to the water's edge.

For long I stood on the beach trying to calm the rage. Then I turned around and slowly made my way up the track, back to my kin. I entered the woods and heard a rustling in the thicket at the edge of the path.

My bearded axe was in my fist. One-handed I swung at the shape moving towards me, and immediately I was rewarded by the muffled sound of a spear shaft clattering onto the hard-packed dirt. I lunged forward and struck out with the haft of my weapon and heard the familiar crunch of wood shattering cartilage. The warrior stumbled backwards. I struck out again, this time with my iron-studded vambrace and the shape crumpled to the ground.

I closed my fist around the stunned man's clothing and dragged him down the path onto the shingles. The waning moon provided enough illumination to identify my attacker as a Gautar, although his armour appeared to be of a higher quality than I had seen before. I noticed that he nursed a grievous spear wound to his leg, explaining why he had fallen behind his comrades.

"Who is your lord?" I hissed, and pressed the blade of my axe against his throat.

"I wish for a quick death in return", he replied.

I nodded.

"I am a ringman of King Haecyn of the Gautar", he said.

"Is Hrethel not your king?" I asked.

"King Hrethel died of grief after the death of his son, Prince Herebeald", the warrior said.

"Who killed Herebeald?" I asked.

"His brother, Haecyn. It was a hunting accident", he said and smiled without humour, revealing bloodstained teeth.

"Sure", I said, and pressed down on the razor-sharp blade.

I walked to the water's edge and collapsed onto the gravel, cradling my head in my hands. Unni's capture left me feeling powerless, swept up in the river of life.

For long I prayed to the one who guided the hand of fate.

Under the light of the waning moon, I listened to the words that came to me, and cut the sacred markings into the haft of my axe.

'The war god from the sea will fall upon the evil king.

Crowing, the ravens will feast on his flesh.'

When I was done, I dipped my fingers into the blood of the warrior and rubbed the corpse-sea into the etchings to draw the attention of the gods.

* * *

Mourdagos lifted the body of a Heruli warrior from the water and laid him on the shingles. "He was a great warrior in his time", the war leader of the Boat Heruli growled and gently stroked the old

111

man's hair. "Sintvalt taught me blade craft – he was like a father to me."

"Any man may take what is mine through the force of his blade - it is his god-given right. But do not steal from me like a coward who comes in the night. The king of the Gautar is a dead man", Mourdagos growled, and I could not help but notice that his right fist was clamped around the sacred golden torque adorning his neck. "We leave at first light", the boat lord added through gritted teeth. "We will row until the blood from our palms drips through the oarlocks. The Gautar will be caught – I swear it by the gods."

When the first golden rays appeared above the eastern horizon, the keels of our four remaining longships cut the dark surface of Lake Mälaren. King Egil had insisted on joining us, accompanied by thirty of his hearthmen.

I stood beside Mourdagos and the erilar, both men's jaws set with determination.

"I care little for the lost treasure of the Svear", Abdarakos said. "But the Gautar have stolen your ship and Ragnar's woman."

"They would not have known that she is my woman. Nor", I added, "that the boats belong to the Heruli."

"You are familiar with our ways, Ragnar", the erilar growled. "Weak men seek excuses. The Heruli care not for that. All that matters is that your woman and my brother's boat have been taken by the Gautar. For that they must die."

Leodis, my Greek tutor, had educated me in the laws of the Roman Empire. The regulations were not easy to understand and justice was difficult to come by. I preferred the ancient ways of the Heruli.

"I agree", I said.

"That is why Attila conquered the world", Abdarakos mused. "Our laws are simple. No scroll is needed. The gods have given every man the knowledge of what is right and what is wrong." He thumped his chest with his fist. "We carry it inside our hearts."

His eye caught the blood runes etched on the haft of my axe.

"I have my own vengeance to wreak", I replied, my words soliciting a slow nod of approval from both men.

Mourdagos signalled the end of the oar shift. I weaved through the rowers and slid in beside Kursik. It took a few heartbeats to feel the rhythm. Then I nodded and he made his way to the prow, where a warrior passed him a mug of ale scooped from a cask.

The pace that Mourdagos set was gruelling. My hands and sinews were rock-hard from working with the axe, spear and bow. Still, at the end of the shift, my back and forearms were on fire and my hands blistered.

Trokondas took the oar from me. "There is nothing like oar-work to toughen one up", he said. "When we catch the Gautar, and we will, none of us will be in a mood for mercy."

Two days we rowed from morning till dusk. My hands were raw, and like Mourdagos had predicted, our blood stained the oarlocks red.

We caught up with our prey mid-morning on the third day, not far south of Runaville. The longships of the Heruli put fear into the hearts of the Gautar, and iron into their backs. For the best part of two hours our bone-weary limbs were unable to close the gap. But then the Gautar tired and we started gaining on them with every stroke.

Asbadus, who was rowing behind me, hissed through his teeth. "They will make for land", he said. "Mark my words."

"Why?" I asked.

"Because on land there are walls to hide behind", he said. "On land, one can run and disappear in the thickets of the dark woods. At sea, there is no place to hide. Here, one's fate is certain."

He had hardly spoken the words when the five Gautar ships turned their prows towards land, heading for a channel between two headlands, which appeared to be the mouth of a river or estuary of sorts.

We were struggling upstream, four hundred paces from the sandy beach where the Gautar had disembarked, when King Haecyn proved that he was no fool. The Gautar put their own ships to the torch and allowed them to float with the current, towards us.

Mourdagos reacted in less than a heartbeat. He shouted commands and the rowers started backing water. One by one the longships reversed course and powered out of the channel while the Gautar ships approached like a wall of flames.

Mourdagos's ship was the last to turn. The searing heat of the floating inferno singed the hair on our arms and legs but we managed to get ahead of the flames and power our way out of the narrow channel into the open sea.

We watched in awe as the blackened hulls disappeared beneath the surface, the water boiling with eruptions of steam. Then Mourdagos issued the commands and we resumed our journey up the channel at an easy pace.

Chapter 15 – Haecyn

Of the Gautar there was no sign.

"I will go to find them", I heard myself say.

"And I will keep him alive", Kursik added, and it was clear that his words were not in jest.

In reply Abdarakos grunted his consent.

During our rushed departure from Uppsala, we had only managed to fit two horses into the crowded boats. While my grandsire's oathsworn saddled the animals, Kursik and I donned our armour and readied our weapons. We strung our horn bows and followed the tracks of the Gautar that led into the greenwood.

I have heard men state that mounted scouts are unable to move silently. To my ears, a man who had lived with the people of the horse, their words are those of fools. A Hun scout on a trained horse can move faster and with more stealth than a man on foot.

We did not follow the dirt track, but turned our horses into the woods, travelling parallel with the path. Kursik led the way, with me following thirty paces behind. Two miles into the forest, the Hun held up an open palm and signalled for me to approach. He gestured in the direction of the path. It took a few heartbeats before I noticed the Gautar warriors, their backs turned to us, crouching close to the shoulder of the track.

On Kursik's signal we moved deeper into the woods, circled around the Gautar ambush, and continued north. Three miles farther we came upon a hillock fortified with a ten-feet high wooden palisade - no doubt the stronghold of some local lord or other. The trees had been cleared for thirty paces around the perimeter. We remained in the forest and watched from the shadows.

"It is a strong position to defend", Kursik admitted reluctantly. "We will lose many men trying to scale the walls."

"I have a plan", I said. "Come, let us return to the erilar with haste."

* * *

When I had given him my words, Abdarakos grinned and slapped my back. "The wolf needs cunning to survive", he said, "not only strength."

While Abdarakos, Mourdagos and King Egil readied their warriors, I led nineteen men down the path at a jog, eager to give effect to my plan. We were a formidable group of warriors as Trokondas, Asbadus, Beremud, Boarex and Kursik all insisted on joining me.

An hour later the twenty of us were shepherded up to the gate of the Gautar hillfort. Our armour smeared with blood, our hands firmly tied behind our backs, and our feet hobbled. Or so it seemed.

Two of Haldr's men led us. They, and ten more of my Svear oathsworn who followed behind the captives, wore the clothes and armour of the Gautar who had intended to ambush us. Earlier, we had ambushed the ambushers and killed them to a man while Boarex and Kursik's arrows made sure none escaped.

I feigned stumbling and collapsed into a heap near the closed gate of the fort. One of Haldr's men kicked me repeatedly while cursing, amongst other things, my mother, drawing great cheers from the Gautar lining the wooden ramparts.

Haldr and his men had lived with the Gautar for years and spoke their tongue perfectly. Fearing they would be recognised as imposters, we had smeared blood on the faces of the men leading the column to act as a disguise. But the gates swung open even before the gatekeepers had spoken to the returning heroes. I feverishly searched for my weapons which were concealed behind my back. My right hand found the haft of my bearded axe and my left tightened around the hilt of my shortsword.

To extend the time until our imminent discovery, Haldr's men stopped at the side of the gate with their backs to the fort, as we had planned, and waved us through.

I stole a glance at the warriors lining the roadway. The man nearest to me took a step closer, spat in my face and drew back his arm in order to throw a punch. His eyes widened for the last time as the blade of my shortsword slid across his neck, opening his veins. The man beside him stumbled backwards, but the blunt end of my bearded axe slammed into his helmetless head and he crumpled to the ground. All around, the Heruli slaughtered the unprepared Gautar.

My eye caught a warrior on the wall walk drawing back his spear. I had to step aside to avoid his tumbling corpse, a Hun shaft embedded in his skull.

While Hun arrows cleared the walls of defenders, the Heruli and Egil's spearmen swarmed through the gate. The Gautar were no match for the wolves of the Heruli and soon there were none of the enemy left to kill. In strength we advanced on the longhouse which stood in the centre of the hillfort. King Haecyn and the last of his hearthmen had barricaded themselves inside in a desperate attempt to escape the slaughter.

The door of the hall burst open and Haecyn emerged, holding Unni in front of him like one would a shield. "I will trade my life for the life of your bride", Haecyn shouted, addressing Egil, of course.

It was not my place to interfere in the negotiations of kings, but I knew that Egil would gladly sacrifice Unni if he could claim the honour of killing the Gautar king. I pushed my way to the back of the crowd of warriors who had gathered to witness the spectacle, where I found Kursik looting corpses and taking scalps. Some habits die hard.

I had always been three inches taller than Kursik, but the toiling and rowing of the past months had broadened my frame. I grabbed the Hun by the arm and in my urgency lifted him off his feet. In the distance I heard Egil shout to Haecyn, "The woman means nothing to me. Kill her if you wish."

"Your bow", I growled.

Kursik, who had focused on the looting, was unaware of the drama playing out eighty paces to the front. But he must have noticed the urgency in my eyes and in one fluid movement he pulled the bow from the case slung over his back and strung it. I gestured to a cart at the side of the path and we leaped onto the rear for elevation.

I had no time to explain, just pointed at the Gautar king.

Kursik was no fool and already had a shaft on the string. He nodded, then released.

The three-bladed tip, given incredible momentum by the horn and sinew bow, entered Haecyn's arm just above the elbow. The heavy Hun arrow shattered the bone and caused the king to stagger backwards, losing his grip around Unni's neck.

To his credit, King Egil responded first. He saw the opportunity, leaped forward, and drove his iron-tipped spear through Haecyn's heart, killing him instantly.

A great cheer erupted from King Egil's hearthmen, who fell on the remainder of the Gautar king's men.

I forced my way through the crowd until I reached Unni, who was bleeding profusely. Kursik's shaft had saved her from Haecyn, but the tip of the arrow had travelled through the flesh and bone of his arm and punctured her chest where it met her shoulder. I cradled her in my arms and pressed my palm against the wound in an attempt to stop the bleeding.

"Leave my woman be, Heruli", I heard a voice say.

I felt the stir of anger deep inside and pressed Unni's palm onto the wound. "Can you hold it?" I whispered into her ear.

"Did you not hear my words, mercenary?" Egil growled again and took a step closer.

Unni nodded in reply to my initial question and I sat her down with her back against the rough oak logs of the hall.

I would like to say that what happened next was the will of the gods, but I realise now that weak men blame the gods for their own actions.

By the time I had laid Unni against the wall I was trembling with anger. I stood to my full height and in the same moment I lashed out at the king of the Svear. My fist caught him squarely on the jaw. He staggered to the rear and fell flat on his back.

The hearthman nearest to the king lunged at me with his spear, but Kursik's broad-bladed arrow slammed into his neck, showering me with a mist of blood. A second oathsworn had committed to defending his lord and he, too, lunged. Boarex's battle-axe whirled through the air and bit deep into the Svear's chest.

Abdarakos had not commanded the great armies of the Scythians and Germani for no reason. When he spoke, men listened – even more so when he spoke in anger.

"Stay your hands, Svearmen", the warlord boomed. The sheer power of his will caused the hearthmen of Egil to freeze in their boots.

"Lay down your spears", he shouted.

Even though my grandsire's command of the local tongue was less than perfect, his tone transcended the barriers of language. As one, the men of the king cast down their spears.

* * *

Abdarakos and Mourdagos waited for us inside the hall of the Gautar.

"We need to get the girl to a healer", Abdarakos growled, and in turn fixed Egil and me with a stare that could curdle milk.

"I suggest we get the woman to Uppsala so Runa and your medicine man can heal her", Egil replied to the erilar's words.

The Svear king turned his gaze on me, but replied to the erilar. "If she chooses to be with him, I will not speak of this again. But if she prefers to be queen of the Svear, I expect you to respect her wish."

123

There was no doubt in my mind that his words were insincere, but Unni's plight was paramount in my thoughts and I nodded.

"We will leave on the morrow", Abdarakos said. "You, Lord King, must depart before nightfall with our best men and the woman. Ragnar is one of them."

"What of my treasure?" he asked, revealing where his true passion lay.

"I will see that the treasure is recovered", Mourdagos said. "The erilar and I will deliver it to Uppsala when we come to take Ragnar home."

I could see that Egil wished to object, but he swallowed back the words and nodded.

When the Svear king had left the hall to make his preparations, Abdarakos clasped me behind the neck and pulled me closer so that our foreheads touched. He kept me close for a span of heartbeats, then nodded and issued a grunt which I construed as a dismissal.

Maybe I imagined it, but I thought I noticed a glint of pride in his good eye.

Chapter 16 – Greed

My mind was so preoccupied with Unni that I failed to give thanks to the gods. But that was not the only mistake I made. I also neglected to expunge the runes from the haft of my axe, which meant that the gaze of the gods did not waver. Looking back, I am sure that the sky-father did avert his gaze, but the eyes of his grimmer kin remained focused on me.

The blood runes can alter the hand of fate, and I still believe that my oversight was the cause of the events that followed.

* * *

I did not notice the blood from my raw palms dripping down the oar, nor did the burning sinews in my back and arms matter to me. The only thing I could think of was to finish my shift so I could care for Unni, who was getting weaker by the hour.

Close to the end of my turn, I noticed Trokondas and Kursik congregate at the steering oar at the stern. For long they engaged in a whispered conversation, frequently pointing at the rising moon.

Trokondas slid in beside me on the chest and gripped the oar to relieve me. "I have spoken to Kursik", he said. "We will continue rowing throughout the night. For the girl, we will do it."

I was too tired to offer a reply and staggered towards the prow where Asbadus was cradling Unni, who was moaning incoherently. He shook his head before I made to take Unni from him. "Lie down, Ragnar", he growled, and there was iron in his voice.

With a bloody palm I stroked Unni's hair, nodded, curled up against the board, and fell into a deep, dreamless sleep.

The first thing I did when I woke was to lick my bloody, chapped lips. The irony taste, accentuated by the saltiness of the sea, caused me to gag. I coughed violently, feeling the pain and tiredness shoot through my limbs.

"I will not", I heard Egil shout at Trokondas, who was still at an oar.

"Let the pup of Abdarakos row", he spat.

"He has rowed more than any man on this ship", Trokondas growled, and I heard the anger in the Isaurian's voice. "All I ask is that you row one shift."

I stood stiffly, pushed past the king, and slipped in beside Trokondas to get into the rhythm of the stroke. The big Isaurian said no more, but I noticed murder in his eyes.

With every stroke of the oar I said a prayer to Ulgin. The sky-father must still have been watching, because the light breeze soon developed into a high wind that howled through the rowlocks, propelling us forward as if Notus, the god of the south wind, pushed at the stern.

The wind continued to gain strength and soon waves crashed into our prow, making it near impossible to steer the ship. There was not a man aboard who did not thank the gods when the steersman managed to turn the ship to the southwest, entering the Bay of Mälaren at the break of dawn.

Lake Mälaren had not escaped the wrath of the summer tempest, but we endured the lashing wind without complaint, knowing that all who remained on the Austmarr would soon be sucked into Njord's weedy deeps.

* * *

Thanks to the wind at the stern, we neared Uppsala late afternoon when the full might of the storm had finally caught up with us. Through the driving rain I spied a lone figure on the shingle beach.

When I heard the familiar sound of the oak hull scraping on gravel, I shipped the oar, vaulted over the board, and landed in the shallows, five paces from where the old shaman leaned on his linden stick.

"She still draws breath" I shouted to Atakam, whose eyes registered no surprise at my words.

The shaman gestured at two horses tied to a nearby ash. "Bring her", he said. "Time is of the essence."

I rode behind Atakam, one hand on the reins, and my right arm wrapped around Unni's waist to make sure that she did not fall from the horse. It felt like an age before we reached the settlement where the shaman directed me to one of the minor halls.

Runa opened the door just as I reached for it. She paid me no heed, but reached for Unni, who was supported between us. "Lay her down, with haste", the old woman said and gestured to a straw-stuffed mattress close to the hearth.

When Unni lay on her back, Runa kneeled down, removed the honey-soaked bandage, and proceeded to clean the wound with boiled linen rags. In the yellow light of the hearth, I could see that Unni's wound had turned an angry red.

"Arrow", Runa growled and beckoned Atakam to approach.

In the land of the Huns and the Scythians, most often, war wounds were caused by arrows. The people of the Sea of Grass had experience treating such injuries, and Atakam, who lived in a time of strife, had seen and tended to hundreds of similar wounds.

The shaman kneeled on the opposite side of the mattress, bent over at the waist, and sniffed the wound. He gave a near imperceptible shake of his head, drew his thin-bladed dagger and held it above the flames.

"When medicine does not work, iron will cure", he mumbled while washing the blade in the flame.

Then he turned to me. "Hold her down", he said, and took a small iron forceps from a pouch and dipped it in vinegar. I recognised the tool – it had been a gift from Leodis the Greek.

I kneeled behind Unni's head and firmly grasped her upper arms in my hands. Atakam cut the wound with the razor-sharp tip of his dagger. I averted my eyes as yellow and red fluid burst from the cut.

"Hold her", he hissed, and started probing the wound with the forceps. Although she was not walking in the world of men, her back arched in pain. Atakam continued unperturbed, and soon held aloft a small shard of wood.

"And that which iron cannot cure, fire will", he said, and immediately I knew what would follow.

Runa extracted a bone-handled cauterising blade from the coals and handed the glowing iron to Atakam, who pressed it onto the bleeding wound. Again, Unni's back arched. She issued a low moan and went limp.

"If fire cannot cure it, nothing will", Atakam said and handed the instrument back to Runa. He turned to face me and I noticed that his eyes were wet.

"I would have rather pressed the iron into my own flesh", he said. "Now I will travel to the realm of the gods and plead for her life", he added, and walked out into the pouring rain.

* * *

Owing to the ministrations of Runa, and Atakam's intervention with the gods, of course, Unni recovered quickly. During this time, King Egil did not visit, nor did he speak of his intended betrothal to her. However, none of us failed to notice the arrival of Svear warriors at Uppsala.

"Egil is planning something", Asbadus said one evening while we were slaking our thirst on a fresh batch of ale. "He has forgotten that Abdarakos was the one who saved his skin from Aun the Old."

"And", Trokondas added, "Egil is yet to reward the erilar for quelling the rebellion of Tonne."

"My grandsire will return with the treasure that the Gautar king has stolen when Unni was taken", I said. "The gold will be sufficient to pay the Heruli and there will be enough left over to satisfy Egil's greed."

One by one, Atakam placed three bone-dry oak logs in the blazing hearth. It took only a handful of heartbeats for the flames to flare up. "I gave the fire that which it desired most", he said.

While the shaman waited for us to think on his words, he drank deeply from his ale horn.

"Greed is like fire", he said. "The more you feed it, the more it wants. Like fire, it destroys all."

* * *

The following morning I sat with Unni while she sipped a thin soup of wild fowl and herbs.

Trokondas strolled into the hall. "A longship approaches, Ragnar", he said. "Come, ride with me."

We made our way south towards the beach, arriving in time to see Mourdagos's longboat slide onto the shingle. While we waited for my grandsire to disembark, we became aware of men approaching from the direction of Uppsala.

King Egil reined in ten paces from us and held up a hand for his hearthmen to stop. "I see that the mercenaries have arrived", he sneered, and gestured with his chin towards the longship. "At least your grandsire values your life enough to return my treasure to me", he added without acknowledging me.

While the crew unloaded the boat, Abdarakos, Mourdagos and a handful of his warriors made their way towards us. I immediately knew something was amiss when I noticed their grim expressions.

Egil, no doubt blinded by his greed, lacked our perceptiveness. "Welcome, warlord", he said when they were still twenty paces away. "Do not unload all my treasure. I have given it much thought – you may keep one part in five."

Abdarakos did not reply until he came to a halt two paces from us. "There is no treasure", he growled. "I have come for my people and my grandson."

The erilar's words had a profound effect on the king, whose face turned bright red. "You speak lies, Herulian", he shouted. "Do you take me for a fool, a dimwit?"

Abdarakos was no one's plaything. He disdained to answer verbally, but in response his hand went to the hilt of his sword. It was clear that he tried his utmost to suppress the rising anger.

Egil, who realised by then that he had overstepped the line, pulled on the reins of his horse and thundered back the way he had come, his guards following at a jog.

"Warn the men", Mourdagos growled. "Today, there will be blood."

I nodded, vaulted onto my horse, and Trokondas and I raced towards our hall.

Chapter 17 – Boar (August 472 AD)

Experience had taught me to heed the words of men like Mourdagos.

Trokondas and I gathered all into the hall where we donned our armour in haste, and strapped on our weapons.

We had hardly finished arming when I heard a commotion outside. I pushed open the door and stepped onto the rough-hewn oak planks of the portico, with Kursik and Trokondas at my side. It came as no surprise that King Egil and his spearmen had surrounded the longhouse. I could not help but notice that, although it was broad daylight, at least four men carried flaming torches.

From our elevated position I spied Abdarakos's approach. The erilar, with Mourdagos at his side, strode at the head of forty Heruli warriors. They came to a halt twenty paces from the king.

"They attacked us while we were recovering your treasure", Mourdagos said. "A new king now leads the Gautar. This one is crafty, but more than that, he is a warrior. He attacked us with overwhelming numbers when we least expected it. Many Heruli sacrificed themselves to allow us to escape."

Abdarakos sighed heavily, and drew his blade from its scabbard. "But you are not a man who listens to reason, are you, King Egil?"

The erilar used his sword to point at the hundred and fifty spearmen surrounding the king. "Now that you have lost your treasure you will seek revenge, even though we have been true to our oath."

Before King Egil could respond, Abdarakos continued. "I will not wait to hear your answer, king, because it matters not", the erilar hissed. "You have sealed your fate by calling me a liar."

The confident sneer vanished from the face of the king as he realised that the words of Abdarakos had turned the tables – the predator had become the prey. He retreated a step and moved into the third rank, secure behind the spears of his hearthmen. But in the heat of the moment, Egil had forgotten about the threat at his rear.

The gods spoke to me then, and I realised that we had one chance to penetrate the line of the foe, and there was only one way to accomplish it.

"Head of the swine", I hissed, and Boarex and Kursik stepped in behind me, their drawn horn bows in their fists. Trokondas, Asbadus and Beremud drew their bearded blades and aligned

135

themselves at the rear of the two Huns. The remainder of our battle-hardened men formed a fourth rank.

"Bar the door", I growled to Atakam, who nodded and complied.

I disregarded the Svear in the two ranks between Egil and me, hefted my axe, and charged.

Before we reached their line, four Hun arrows slammed into the hearthmen in front of me. The dying men staggered backwards, throwing the second rank into disarray. The man facing me drew back his spear, but I trusted my armour and laid on a burst of speed. This caught him unawares and unable to wield his weapon. I slammed into his shield with my shoulder, my axe drawn back, pushing him into the warrior behind him. I rotated my hips, and the blade of my axe came around with tremendous force, split the man's shield, and bit deep into his arm. Kursik and Beremud chose that moment to release their arrows, which slammed into the men beside the warrior with the ruined arm.

The Svear ranks had buckled under our charge, but they outnumbered us many times over. I saw a wide-eyed Egil only one rank away from my blade, but by then the foe had come to grips with the situation and I felt the impact as a spear strike ripped scales from my armour. I had gambled all on reaching Egil with the initial attack, but it had failed. I realised then that only the intervention of the gods could save us. I swung wildly at the men facing me, but could not keep all the foes at bay. A spear snaked past my defences and scored a burning cut along my side. In desperation I severed the shaft of the spear, and my thumb dragged across the runes I had cut into the haft of my bearded axe.

Another Svear blade struck like a viper and it felt as if a hot poker was thrust into the flesh of my shoulder. Involuntarily my fist tightened around the haft of my axe, and I could feel the god-markings underneath my fingers – I swear to this day that I sensed the gods changing my fate.

When I looked up again, the Svear who had pierced my armour was no longer there, and I stared into Egil's gaping mouth, from which the tip of a blade erupted.

The evil king crumpled to the ground and I came face to face with Abdarakos.

"The king is dead", I boomed, which caused a ripple through the ranks of the Svear. The spearmen stepped back, as if awaiting a command from a higher power.

At that moment the door of the longhouse burst open and Runa strode forth. The old seer leaned on her linden stick and shouted the words, her voice tinged with an unearthly quality, "The gods have spoken, Svearmen. Lower your spears and retire to the

137

warriors' hall. I will care for the dead and wounded. Defy the gods, and you will be cursed for eternity."

All Svear knew that the medicine woman communed with the gods. As one they turned their backs to the Heruli and returned to their hall.

* * *

When Atakam had finished binding our wounds, I collapsed beside the hearth.

I was not prepared to risk a repeat of the day's events and used the blade of my dagger to scrape the god whispers from the haft of my axe. When I was done, I cast the fine wood shavings into the fire. A puff of white smoke erupted from the hearth and disappeared into the night sky.

Atakam met my gaze and nodded his approval.

Just then, Unni handed me a horn brimming with golden mead and sat down beside me. "You could be king of the Svear", she whispered, which caused me to choke on the delicious brew.

"The Svear will need a strong man to be king", Runa said, echoing Unni's words.

From the far side of the hearth, Mourdagos and Abdarakos listened with interest, their eyebrows raised.

Rather than to answer immediately, I drank deeply from the horn, allowing the mead to wash over my mind. For long I remained silent, then took another sip and shook my head.

"No", I said. "The Svear is not ready to be ruled by a Heruli. The Svear need a Svearman to be their king."

"But what of the threat of the Danes and the Gautar?" Abdarakos replied bluntly. "The Svear have little experience of war."

"That", I replied, "is why you, grandfather, must become the war leader of the Svear."

"And who will be their king?" Abdarakos asked. "I thought that Egil did not leave an heir."

Runa issued a grunt, rose from her place beside the hearth, and strode from the hall.

"Where is she going?" Abdarakos asked.

"Patience is a virtue", Atakam replied, confirming my suspicion that he and the old woman had conspired.

While we waited for Runa to return, Atakam re-enacted the battle of the day, telling of how the evil king had been killed. He went down on all fours, mimicking how Egil was vanquished by the head of the boar.

We raucously cheered the performance, and afterwards all shouted their insistence that the shaman repeat the act.

Atakam was saved by Runa who entered the hall, a young warrior at her side.

"Who is this?" Abdarakos asked, gesturing at the young man.

"This is Othere, the son of Egil", Runa replied.

"How did you manage to find an heir so soon?" the erilar asked, a frown creasing his brow.

"It was easy", Runa replied in the tongue of the Heruli. "I chose one from the long list of bastards King Egil has sired", she added, and offered the grinning boy a gap-toothed smile.

* * *

On the night of the full moon, Othere was sworn in as the king of the Svear.

Two nights later, the new king attended my wedding ceremony. In a way it was more than just the bonding of two people – it also symbolized the bonding of two peoples, the Svear and the Heruli.

My grandsire, the scarred, one-eyed warlord, agreed to be the erilar, the war leader of the king. In return, on the insistence of the elders, Abdarakos was made a lord of the Svear, and granted great swathes of land surrounding Runaville. No longer were the Heruli guests on the distant shores of Scandza, they had become kin of the Svear.

Mourdagos accompanied us on our return journey to the fort at Runaville, and started making preparations to return to the lands of the Boat Heruli.

We all believed that we had achieved that which we had set out to do. We had obeyed the gods, defied the odds, and carved out a home in a foreign land, far from the machinations of Rome and the Germanic kingdoms surrounding the great Empire.

While we basked in our success, the gods were watching. And, of course, laughing, because we had no way of knowing what they had in store for us. Our journey had not come to an end, it had barely begun.

And then, on a foggy, late summer morning, a longship arrived.

Chapter 18 – Longship (September 472 AD)

"The emperor of the West is dead", Ottoghar said, and took a swallow of ale. "And he died by my blade", the Scirii prince added, eliciting gasps from Abdarakos and Mourdagos.

"Were you forced to flee for your life?" I asked.

"No", the prince said and waved away my concern. "I executed the emperor on the instructions of Ricimer, the high general of the West."

Mourdagos sensed that there was a tale involved. He reached for Ottoghar's empty horn and refilled it to the brim. "Tell us", the big man said.

The prince nodded in reply and told his tale.

"When you departed for the North last year, I returned to Rome with a host of warriors from the Rugii, Scirii and Heruli, only to find that Leo, the Eastern Emperor, had sent General Olybrius to mediate between Ricimer and Anthemius."

"I have heard the name of Olybrius", Abdarakos said. "The men of the tribes speak highly of him. He is a man of virtue who treats our kind with respect."

"Initially, the negotiations were a success", Ottoghar continued. "So much so that I was planning to send the warriors back to their respective tribal lands."

"But something happened?" Abdarakos asked.

Ottoghar nodded. "Indeed", he confirmed. "Ricimer is no fool. He stationed men at all the gates of the city as well as at the harbour. One of the guards, a Herulian warrior, searched an imperial messenger when he disembarked in the harbour at Ostia."

Ottoghar lowered his voice as if imparting a secret, and all leaned in. "A concealed letter from Leo, the Eastern Emperor, to his lapdog, Anthemius, was found."

Abdarakos slapped the tabletop and leaned back. "I knew it", he proclaimed.

"And", Ottoghar continued in a whisper. "Leo instructed Anthemius to kill Ricimer."

All around the table men gasped at the revelation, but Ottoghar raised a hand to stall a response. "There is more", he said. "Leo also instructed Anthemius to kill Olybrius, the mediator."

I shook my head in disgust. "It sounds more and more like a scheme concocted by Zeno", I said. "He is the man who tricked us into killing Aspar."

"It matters not", Ottoghar said. "Aspar was a Goth, he deserved to die."

"What happened then?" Mourdagos asked.

"Anthemius hid behind the walls of Rome, but Ricimer soon cut off his supplies from the river. Both men summoned their allies from Gaul, and after a long siege a great battle was fought, from which Ricimer emerged victorious. Anthemius should have done the honourable thing and fallen on his sword, but he dressed in the robes of a beggar and tried to flee in secret."

"Coward", Abdarakos growled, followed by nods from around the table.

"He was caught hiding in a holy place", Ottoghar confirmed. "And I took his head as a reward for his treachery."

"So why are you here?" Abdarakos asked.

Ottoghar pursed his lips. "There is more", he said.

"The Longobardi are moving south yet again", he said. "Ricimer believes that Leo has incited them to invade the lands of the Scirii and the Heruli. It is his way of robbing Ricimer of his warriors and his power."

"You have not told me why you are here", Abdarakos said, fixing Ottoghar with a stare.

"I come at the behest of Rodolph, the man who tried to kill you, Lord Abdarakos", the Scirii prince replied.

For a time all were too shocked to speak.

Then Abdarakos stood from his seat, the chair rattling onto the flagstones. "Do not speak his name again in my presence", the erilar growled, his fist gripping the hilt of his sword.

Ottoghar raised both hands to placate my grandfather. "You and my father fought side by side. For his sake, hear me out, lord", he pleaded. "After that I will not mention Rodolph's name again, ever."

It took at least a hundred heartbeats for the erilar to calm himself. Then he sighed in resignation, picked up the chair, and sat down again. "Your father was my friend, my brother. I owe him that much."

Ottoghar inclined his head, acknowledging the enormity of Abdarakos's concession. "I have little respect for Rodolph, the self-styled king of the Heruli, lord", he said. "But I endure him because I need his warriors to keep the Goths and the East Romans at bay. It is worth the sacrifice."

Abdarakos issued a grunt of agreement and gestured for Ottoghar to continue.

"Rodolph is a fool", the Scirii prince sneered. "He believed that he could make peace with the Longobardi, but he was wrong. Aldihoc, their king, has already driven the remnants of the Scirii from their lands. Rodolph did not lift a finger to assist my people, in the hope that his apathy would pacify the Longobardi."

"Now King Aldihoc has turned his gaze to the south, to the lands of the Heruli, and King Rodolph trembles with fear. Many of the warriors have deserted Rodolph's banner and hire out their sword arms to the highest bidder in faraway lands."

"Rodolph knows that there is only one man who can save the Heruli from the dark fate that he has brought down upon the tribe, and that man, Lord Abdarakos, is you. The tales of your deeds are told around the cooking fires when the sun sets. If you agree to lead the Heruli, the warriors will flock to your banner for the privilege to fight by your side. I, for one, and all those who have fought beside my father, will join you."

146

Abdarakos was visibly moved by the words of the Scirii prince. "I will think on it, Prince Ottoghar", he said. "But you are our guest, and now we will feast in your honour."

As the evening progressed, the ale took its toll. While Ottoghar was sharing a tale with the erilar's hearthmen, I found myself alone with Mourdagos and Abdarakos. Weighed down by the imminent decision, both men had taken ale in moderation.

"What say you, Ragnar?" Abdarakos asked.

Requesting my counsel was a compliment, but I felt intimidated nonetheless.

"Rodolph will try to kill you again", I said, and to my own ears I sounded as cynical as Kursik. "As soon as his fear of the Longobardi disappears, his greed and jealousy will get the better of him."

The erilar grunted his agreement and gestured for me to continue.

"Nonetheless, we are honour bound to assist our people", I replied. "But Rodolph must die", I concluded.

The expression on his face told me that Abdarakos agreed with my assessment. He turned his gaze to Mourdagos, who said, "I concur with Ragnar, brother. I pledge four thousand warriors in support of your cause."

"But", the big man added, "the Boat Heruli will not fight against their kin."

"Thank you, brother", Abdarakos replied. "We will not redden our blades with the blood of our kin. You have my oath."

"How will you rid the world of Rodolph then?" Mourdagos asked.

"I know not", the erilar replied with a shrug, although I thought I noticed a glint in his good eye.

* * *

The following morning after breaking our fast, Abdarakos called all the men of consequence to his hearth.

"I have come to a decision", he said. "We will answer your call, Prince Ottoghar, subject to one condition."

Abdarakos raised a hand to show that he was not done. "We need to decide who will travel with us and who will stay. Fate has brought me to the lands of the Svear and I intend to return to this hall if the gods will it. My place is no longer amongst the Heruli. I have become a relic of a bygone age."

"Asbadus and I have spoken", Trokondas said. "We will travel south with you, but continue east once we reach the lands of the Heruli. I need to be at my brother Illus's side now that Ragnar has married. I believe that the gods sent me to this distant shore for a reason, but I have completed my task."

Trokondas's words filled me with sadness, but I had known all along that one day he would return to his people.

"The gods wish for me to accompany you, erilar", Atakam whispered.

"I will be at your side as always", Sigizan said, but the shaman shook his head.

"No Sigizan", he said. "You belong here. This is our home and we cannot allow the Gautar to destroy it during our absence."

Sigizan made to protest, but the old shaman added, "It is the will of the gods."

Runa, who was also seated at the table, spoke then. "Ragnar, you must accompany the erilar."

I had only recently been reunited with Unni and had no plan of leaving. Her words hit me like a spear in the gut, and I am sure I gasped in surprise.

"But you told me that my destiny lies in this land?" I said, and to my own ears my words sounded like that of a coward.

Runa saved me from embarrassment. "I know you wish to protect Unni and me", she said, "but the time for you to settle here has not yet arrived. Go with your grandsire and save your people."

"I am with Ragnar", Kursik said. "Whatever he decides."

"As am I", Boarex added.

"I will follow Ragnar", Beremud, the big Goth, growled.

With all eyes on me, I had little choice than to acquiesce, although my mind raced in panic about what I would tell Unni.

Abdarakos grunted his agreement. "Good, then it is settled."

"What is the condition that you spoke of, lord?" Ottoghar asked, his eyes narrow.

Mourdagos slapped the prince's shoulder with a meaty paw as he rose from his seat. "I have asked Abdarakos the same question", the big man said and turned to face the erilar. "Tell him what you told me, brother."

"Trust me, Prince Ottoghar. I will tell you what the condition is as soon as we have departed", my grandsire said, and dismissed us with a wave of his hand.

Chapter 19 – Dream

"I don't know how I am going to explain this to Unni", I told Runa after we had stepped from the hall, hoping to receive wise counsel. But rather than provide me with sage advice, the old seer doubled over at the waist, cackling with laughter.

Runa struggled to regain her composure. I, on the contrary, failed to see the humour in the situation.

"It was Unni who told me that the gods would send you on a quest", she said. "She dreamed about it."

"Why didn't she tell me?" I asked.

"She didn't know how to", Runa replied, her voice laced with sarcasm.

I scowled in reply and lengthened my stride.

* * *

Although Ottoghar wished to depart before winter, the gods decided otherwise. One storm rolled in on the back of another, so much so that only a madman would have risked Ran's wrath by taking the whale-path across the Austmarr.

I knew that I would be gone for months, if not years. The time that I did not toil in the forest, work to strengthen ramparts, or train with spear, sword and bow, I spent with Unni. We explored the countryside on horseback, and most times I returned with a deer or boar for the pot. When the snow came, we huddled around the fire. Atakam told us stories about Ulgin and the gods of the Sea of Grass while Runa shared tales of the deities of the Svear. Abdarakos told us of the exploits of the great khan, Attila. Trokondas, Asbadus, Boarex and I spoke about our time at the East Roman court.

Apart from the physical attraction, Unni and I grew as close as sword brothers. I found that I started to dread the coming of spring when the violent storms of the Austmarr would abate.

But the gods ignored my plea, and the snow finally melted. Just before high tide on a chilly morning early in April, when Ran and her daughters were finally appeased, we cast off. I struggled to find the rhythm of the stroke, focusing on Unni waving at me from the beach. I drew much comfort from the fact that Sigizan, Haldr and most of Abdarakos's oathsworn stood beside her on the shingle. To bolster our defences, fifty of Mourdagos's best warriors remained. Apart from being a great champion and a strategist, Sigizan was nobody's fool, and I knew that the ringfort at Runaville would not easily fall into enemy hands.

"So, what is the condition that you spoke of?" I heard Ottoghar ask Abdarakos when the beach finally disappeared from view and we settled into the rhythm of the stroke.

"If we survive this quest, you, Prince Ottoghar, will be the war leader of the Heruli", the erilar said. "The tribe has no need of a king."

My grandsire's words wiped the grin from the Scirii prince's lips. "Me? I am no Heruli. They will never accept me."

"When the Longobardi have been subjugated, I will make sure that the glory accrues to you, Prince Ottoghar", Abdarakos said. "You will then be able to fill the void left by Rodolph's death."

"But Rodolph lives", Ottoghar said, his eyes narrowing.

"Not for long", the erilar growled. "Did you really think that I would disregard the fact that he tried to kill us?"

"What about the Heruli's plight?" Ottoghar asked.

"Rest assured, Prince Ottoghar", my grandsire said. "I am old enough to stay my hand until we have dealt with the Longobardi."

Ottoghar did not reply, but stared into the blue.

After two hundred heartbeats had passed, Abdarakos placed his hand on the prince's shoulder. "Do you accept my condition?" he asked.

"Do I have a choice?" Ottoghar asked.

"No", Abdarakos replied, "but neither did I."

* * *

We crossed the Austmarr without incident and, for many days, made our way along the coast to the place where the River Trave spilled into the sea. Pharus, the old steersman, expertly guided us around submerged sandbanks and rocks that would rip apart even the stoutest of oak hulls. The other ships followed in our wake like ducklings would their mother.

Mourdagos, who stood beside Abdarakos, wore a broad grin as we neared the home of the Boat Heruli. "Why do you look so happy, Uncle?" I asked. "You have gained little treasure, apart from the tales."

Mourdagos appeared decidedly guilty, and exchanged glances with Abdarakos.

"Tell him", my grandsire said.

"Do you remember Egil's treasure that was stolen by the Gautar?" the big man asked.

I nodded.

"It is true that their new king, Hygelac, caught us unawares and as a result we lost the treasure – some of it anyway. But most of the gold and silver made it into our hull."

In response to my frown, he raised a placating hand. "We knew that Egil had to die, Ragnar", he said. "He wished for the hand of your woman. Would you have allowed him to take her?"

"And", he added, "what use does a dead man have for gold?"

"I have given my share of the treasure to Mourdagos", Abdarakos said and slapped his brother-in-law's back. "Will it not be unfair to expect him to carry the cost of the warriors that he will send to our aid?"

Without waiting for an answer, he added, "Your share I have left with Runa and Unni", he said. "To spend as they see fit."

"When I return, it will be as a poor man", I said, "although, at least, I will have a happy woman."

Mourdagos draped his oak-like arm around my shoulders. "Let me share a secret", he said, and lowered his voice. "A happy wife is worth more than all the treasure in the world."

155

* * *

We spent only one night in the camp of the Boat Heruli, midway between the Trave and the mighty Elbe River, twenty miles to the south.

The following morning Mourdagos escorted us to where his longships were moored close to the northern bank of the Elbe. He gestured to the old steersman who was inspecting a smaller boat, pulled up on the muddy bank. "Pharus will guide you downstream", the big man said. "When the flow of the river turns south, stay away from the eastern bank. Longobardi vermin infest the woods", he added, and spat in the mud to emphasize his point.

When Mourdagos had said his goodbyes, he embraced me in a bear hug, then pressed his forehead to mine. "Take care of the old man, Ragnar", he whispered. "He is as much a brother to me as you are a son."

* * *

The longship was small but sturdy – clinker-built from oak, and well riveted. The strong smell of pine resin and raw wool confirmed my suspicion that the hull had recently been caulked. She had four oars on a side, meaning that we required eight rowers per shift. Abdarakos and Atakam would row only in a time of crisis, so Mourdagos sent us nine of his warriors to pull oars.

Pharus, the weathered steersman, waited until the current turned before casting off. We rowed south and west on the back of a flood tide, effortlessly gliding across the smooth surface of the Elbe.

Abdarakos gestured to the distant banks. "To the north and east lie the lands of the Saxons, to the south and west the Thuringians", he said. "Both tribes are our allies. Many of Mourdagos's warriors who bear the mark of the Heruli are of Saxon blood."

For eight days we made our way upriver, camping on the forested banks when evening came. Once or twice our path crossed with a band of Thuringian warriors. The markings on our cheeks identified us as allies and we traded for food and trinkets without incident.

On the ninth day the flatlands slowly gave way to hills. By late afternoon we rowed through a deep ravine, the shadowy banks overgrown with ancient oaks and hornbeams.

Abdarakos gestured to the eastern bank where a long-fallen forest giant had created a clearing of sorts. The kindling close to the bank was damp, so while the others set up camp, the erilar, Atakam, Ottoghar and I ventured higher up the slope to collect firewood. My three companions pointed out the logs they wanted, and my axe cut the long, dry branches down to size.

We were no more than three hundred paces from camp when a high-pitched moan split the silence. All froze in their tracks, as few men did not immediately recognise the presence of a brown bear. I had hardly recovered my wits when the yelps, growls and whimpering of a wolf pack on the hunt reached my ears.

Atakam gestured for us to follow him and we carefully made our way towards the moss-covered bole of a fallen oak, overgrown with shrubs and ferns. We crouched down behind the obstacle and peered at the scene playing out less than fifty paces away.

A pack of wolves had managed to corner a monster of a male bear against a cliff face. Usually, wolves know better than to attack a bear, especially such a large and powerful animal, because of its ability to kill or maim with a single blow from a clawed paw. But although the scarred bear had once been the master of the forest, it was old as well as injured. Its right front leg must have been broken, as it could not put its weight upon it while it fended off the snarling, biting wolves with difficulty.

A large black wolf had had enough and, seeing an opportunity, went for the jugular. But its mighty jaws failed to penetrate the thick furry folds of the bear's neck. The beast shook off its attacker and smashed it aside with a giant paw, tearing open the wolf's stomach and leaving the dying animal whimpering as its lifeblood seeped into the damp earth.

Another wolf, a grey, attacked when he saw the bear mutilate its kin. The bear was deceptively fast and the beast's jaws closed around the grey's neck. With an audible snap the wolf's spine was severed and the bear cast the lifeless carcass to the side as if it were a rag.

For long the remaining wolves kept up their attack, taking no more than mouthfuls of bear fur from time to time.

Atakam pointed to a large wolf at the far side. "The white one is the leader of the pack", he said. "It is trying to understand the weakness of the bear. Only then will it attack."

Just when we thought that the wolves would abandon their quest, the white wolf joined the fray, charging the bear like a streak of lighting. It did not strike at the jugular, but sunk its yellow teeth into the bear's injured leg, just above the paw.

The beast roared in pain and reared up onto its hind legs, lifting its attacker into the air. But the white did not release its grip. So focused was the bear on the leader of the pack and its injured leg that it allowed the rest of the wolves to gain a grip on its hind legs. The white released its jaws, fell to the ground and jumped to the side, dodging the swipe from the bear's healthy paw. The bear's hind legs, weakened by the other wolves, buckled, and it fell onto its side.

The white was waiting for the opportunity, sprang forward, and ripped open the throat of the beast. With a mournful bellow the bear breathed its last, and its giant head slumped to the leaf-covered ground.

We were too overawed to speak. Eventually the shaman gestured for us to follow him. He walked two hundred paces down the hill, in the direction of the camp. Then he halted and lowered himself onto the leaves, indicating that we should join him.

"This is no coincidence", Atakam said. "It is a sign from the gods."

None of us had even heard of a bear being killed by wolves, never mind witnessed it. Only a fool would think that it was not fate.

"The bear is a mighty beast", Abdarakos said. "It knows no equal in the forest realm. None are able to stand against its might. But it is old, injured, weakened and tired."

"The bear is the Western Roman Empire", Ottoghar hissed, his eyes wide. "And the tribes are the wolves."

The shaman stared at the prince intently and grunted his agreement.

"But although the bear appeared weak, it was still a powerful enemy", I mused. "It was still able to kill its attackers with impunity – the ones who acted in haste."

"But the white wolf, the leader, the wise one, triumphed", Atakam whispered. "Why?" he asked, his gaze still fixed on Ottoghar.

"Because it knew the bear's weakness", he said. "And the white wolf waited for an opportune moment."

"Good", the shaman said, and stiffly rose to his feet. "Learn from it, then", he added before he turned to walk away.

There was no mistaking that his words were meant for the ears of Ottoghar.

Chapter 20 – Vitava (April 473 AD)

On the insistence of Pharus, we departed before sunrise the following morning. "Where the Wild River, the Vitava, spills into the Elbe, there is a small settlement", he said. "It will be good if we were to reach it while it is still light."

"Why?" Abdarakos asked.

"Ale and mead, lord", Pharus said, and issued a gap-toothed smile.

The erilar grinned in response. "Then you had better tell that to the men who pull the oars", he said.

Mid-morning, while the mist still lingered on the water, it started to drizzle. Late afternoon, when we spied the three longhouses close to the southern bank, we were soaked to the bone, tired and thirsty.

We pulled the boat onto the riverbank and tied it to an ash mooring post. The erilar commanded two of Mourdagos's men to take the first watch. At first they appeared downcast until he uttered the magic words. "Tonight I will pay for a bowl of hot pottage and all the mead and ale you can drink. You will be relieved in an hour."

At the expense of a few silvers, Abdarakos purchased a dry place near the hearth to spread our furs, a bowl of pottage each, and enough ale and mead for all.

Fisud, the greybeard who owned the inn, if it could be called that, was a Thuringian who had fought under the banner of Attila. When he became aware of the identity of Abdarakos and Ottoghar, he promptly refunded the erilar's coin.

"I will not take silver from the man who saved my skin more times than I care to remember, lord", he said. "And it is a great honour to have a prince of our kin, the Scirii, under my roof."

Abdarakos held up a hand. "We will not enjoy your hospitality and food without payment."

But Fisud would not budge. "When people hear that Abdarakos of the Heruli and Prince Ottoghar had spent a night in my hall, they will flock from far and wide to sample my pottage and ale", he said. "I am the one who will profit from your stay."

Once we had eaten our fill of the rich boar, herb and root pottage, Fisud joined us at the table.

"I could not help to hear the men speak of your journey", he said cautiously. "Only yesterday the first travellers of spring who came from the south brought dark tidings. Do you wish to know?"

163

"Tell us", Ottoghar said.

"The man who ruled Rome is dead", Fisud said, and stared at us expectantly.

Ottoghar waved away his words. "I killed him with my own hands", he said. "Surely you must have heard as much?" he added, and took a deep swallow from his cup.

For five heartbeats the innkeeper's brow wrinkled in utter confusion, then he seemed to come to a realisation. "You travel from the far north, don't you, lord?" he asked.

Ottoghar nodded.

"Then you wouldn't know", Fisud said.

"Know what?" Ottoghar asked, the irritation clearly discernible in his voice.

"Lord Ricimer, the man who ruled Rome, is dead, lord", he said.

Ottoghar's cup dropped to the floor and his complexion turned ashen, but he otherwise held his composure. He grabbed Fisud's wrist, who had rushed to clean up the spilled ale.

"Tell me what you know, innkeeper", Ottoghar growled.

The greybeard gestured to a serving girl. "First, a full cup for the prince", he said and retook his seat.

164

"After Emperor Anthemius's er, … demise, Ricimer appointed Olybrius as emperor of the West."

"That, I know", Ottoghar said.

"Ricimer died sometime in August last year, two months after Anthemius", he said. "Then Emperor Olybrius died in October, two months later."

Ottoghar rose from his seat, his hand on his sword. "It cannot be", he said, eyeing the innkeeper with suspicion. "You are a spinner of lies."

Fisud suddenly appeared decidedly nervous. "I speak the truth, lord", he said and raised both his palms.

Abdarakos clamped his fist around Ottoghar's arm. "Sit down", he growled. "Let us give the man time to tell his tale."

Fisud acceded with a nod and told us all. Notwithstanding the distrust of Ottoghar, it was soon apparent that the innkeeper spoke true.

Both Ricimer and Olybrius had purportedly died of natural causes. But I had spent enough time at the East Roman court to know that it is highly likely that they had been murdered. Such was the way of the Romans.

Later that evening, when it was my turn to guard the boat, Atakam volunteered to join me.

We sat in silence for long before he cleared his throat. "Ragnar, do you recall the bear and the wolves?"

"I think about little else", I replied.

"Rome is weakening, and soon the wolves will descend. But careful they must be", he said with a snicker, "the bear will rip apart the hasty ones."

* * *

The prow of the longship cleaved the thin mist that lingered atop the grey water. There was no sign of the dark clouds of the day before and the skies were clear and blue.

Pharus leaned on the steering oar and the boat gently swerved to the south, entering the mouth of the Vitava.

Ottoghar gestured to the eastern bank. "King Flaccitheus of the Rugii is the master of these lands", he said. "Many of the Rugii are moving south across the Danube to the Roman province of Noricum. There they man the walls and forts and fight side by side with the Romans."

166

"Who do the Romans fight against?" I asked. "Since they are at peace with the Rugii."

"The Ostrogoths", Ottoghar said and spat over the side of the boat. "Theodemir, their king, is forever mounting raids against the farmers of Noricum. Even Saint Severinus, the holy man of Noricum, has little time for them."

"The Longobardi know that the Rugii are moving south", he continued, and again gestured to the eastern bank. "They exploit this and are slowly infiltrating these lands. They send raiding parties that destroy Rugian farms and then skulk back across the Elbe."

"Why do the Rugii not simply cross the Danube and take Noricum?" I asked.

"Because the bear can still bite", he said, "and I am its teeth."

The prince had hardly finished speaking when an arrow, arcing from the eastern bank, slammed into the portside board of the longship. The rowers ducked, protected by their shields fastened against the side.

Prince Ottoghar leaned over the side and broke the shaft of the arrow. He studied the fletching. "Longobardi filth", he spat.

Slowly we made our way south along the Vitava, deeper into the lands of Flaccitheus, until, on the afternoon of the fourth day, we arrived at our destination – the stronghold of the Rugii. After Abdarakos had made arrangements for Pharus and his crew, we sent a message to the king.

An hour before the sun set, Prince Ferderuchus, the second son of the king, arrived. Ottoghar and I had fought side by side with the prince and shared the bond of the warrior. Once the introductions had been made, he embraced us like brothers. "It is good to see you", he said. "We have been expecting you."

"Expecting us?" Abdarakos asked. "How can that be?"

"Come see for yourself, lord", Ferderuchus said, and gestured for us to follow him.

Abdarakos, Atakam, Ottoghar and I accompanied the prince to the great hall of the king of the Rugii.

The fierce guards blocking the door stepped aside when the prince approached.

King Flaccitheus, wrapped in furs, rose from his chair when we entered. "Abdarakos!" he shouted, and all but ran to embrace my grandsire. "I feared that I would never share a horn with you again in this life."

After the old king had greeted us, he invited us to take seats. Only then did I notice a man sitting cross-legged on the floor at the far side of the hearth. He was gaunt, dressed only in a thin tunic of undyed linen. My first thought was that he was a slave, but a heartbeat later recognition dawned on me.

"Lord Severinus", I said, and inclined my head to the Apostle of Noricum.

The old priest slowly came to his feet. "Ragnar, the young Scourge of God", he said with a thin smile. Severinus then turned to face my companions and inclined his head. "You, lord, must be the great warlord of the Heruli. Your reputation precedes you, Lord Abdarakos."

"Tribune Flavius Odovaker", Severinus said, and it was clear that the old man was fond of the prince.

The frail holy man then turned his gaze on Atakam. "The seer of the great khan", he said in passable Germani. "I pray that God will show you the error of your ways, shaman. Maybe one day we will be able to serve the same God."

"I will sacrifice to Ulgin for the same result", Atakam replied earnestly. The two holy men held each other's gaze for a span of heartbeats. I could not help but feel like a blind man among the sighted.

Ottoghar broke the standoff. "I heard that Ricimer and Olybrius have departed."

Severinus tore his gaze away from Atakam. "Before he died, Ricimer appointed prince Gundobad of the Burgundians as his successor, as high general of the West", he said. "And Gundobad raised Senator Glycerius to the purple."

"Is Gundobad as formidable as Ricimer?" Abdarakos asked.

"Who knows", the holy man said. "Gundobad has turned his back on Rome. He has returned to the land of his fathers to take the crown."

"In less than a year they have all gone", Ottoghar mused. "Anthemius, Ricimer, Olybrius and Gundobad."

"I told you that the Lord would remove the obstacles from your path, did I not?" Severinus replied.

Ottoghar frowned in response, but before the prince could offer a reply, Flaccitheus interrupted. "Father Severinus has come to my court to warn us of a grave danger."

Chapter 21 – Threat

The king's words served to capture our attention.

"It is the Goths", Flaccitheus sighed. "Fifteen years ago, the emperor of the East allowed them to settle in Pannonia. Like a plague of locusts, they have consumed the wealth of the land. First, they raided the farms of the Romans. When none remained, they survived on the annual tribute from the coffers of the Eastern Empire. But the gold of the East now goes to the Thracian Goths. The Pannonian Goths need plunder to survive, as they have lost the desire to till the soil."

Flaccitheus turned to Severinus. "Tell them, holy father", he said.

"Theodemir and his brother Vidimir, the two Goth chieftains, are gathering their people. They are preparing for a great migration", Severinus said. "There is a rumour that the Ostrogoths will move west to take Italia from the Romans."

"To my ears it sounds like a problem for the Romans", Abdarakos growled.

"Alas, many thousands of Rugii have settled in Noricum, south of the Danube", Flaccitheus replied. "If the Goths turn west, they will not only devour Roman Noricum, but Rugiland as well.

There is no denying it – the fate of the Rugii is bound to that of Noricum."

"The wolves are smelling the weakness of the great bear", Atakam said. "The one who locks its jaws around the throat of Rome will take the lion's share of the spoils."

Flaccitheus nodded his agreement with the shaman, then turned to the erilar. "I wish to ask you a favour, brother", the king said.

Abdarakos issued a grunt of consent.

"If there is one man who can sway the opinion of Theodemir, it is you, Abdarakos", he said. "You taught him all he knows. To you he will listen. Persuade him to invade the East and to leave the lands of the Rugii untouched."

"I will do as you ask", Abdarakos replied without hesitation.

Flaccitheus eyed the erilar with caution. "Then I suppose I should ask what you wish for as recompense", the king said, and gestured for a slave to refill our cups.

"I will ask you for a favour in return", Abdarakos said.

Flaccitheus held up an open palm to stall the words of the erilar. "I grant it", he said, "whatever it is, as long as it is within my power to do so. When the countless horde of the Ostrogoths come west, the Rugii will cease to exist. If you can dissuade them, there is nothing that I would not do in order to repay you."

"But no more talk of Goths", he said and held out his horn for a refill.

"Let us eat, drink and be merry", he said. "For life is short."

Severinus, the Apostle of Noricum, was not a man of excess. He rose from his seat, no doubt preferring to spend the evening in solitude, praying to his God. But he must have been weak from fasting and cold, and I noticed the telltale signs of a man about to faint.

I took hold of his arm. "I will help you to your quarters, father", I said, adopting the term that the Christians use to address their priests.

We made our way to Severinus's rooms, fifty paces from the great hall of the king. Hidden by the shadows, I helped him up the steps of his quarters. Just then, a beautiful woman passed us by, flanked by two burly guards.

"Gisa", he sighed. "She is a wicked and sinister one", he said, "as God is my witness."

"Even more sinister than a heathen like me, lord?" I asked when she had passed.

"Of course not", he said, "you are worse by far", and gently patted my arm with his bony fingers while pushing open the door with his other hand. In the yellow lamplight I thought that I noticed a smile play around the corners of his mouth.

* * *

On the morrow, Abdarakos, Ottoghar, Boarex, Kursik, Trokondas, Beremud, Asbadus and I departed from the Rugii stronghold. Flaccitheus's second son, Prince Ferderuchus, had volunteered to join us. We would head south through the lands of the Rugii, then cross the Danube and make our way east along the main Roman road to Pannonia.

I was curious as to who the wife of Feva was, and asked the Scirii prince while we were adjusting the tack of our horses.

"Gisa is the daughter of Vidimir", Ottoghar said and swung up into the saddle.

"To me she is no more than an evil bitch", Prince Ferderuchus replied from atop his black gelding. "She will try her best to hasten the death of my father, the king. When Flaccitheus is no more, she will rule through my weak brother, Feva, who will be king."

"Theodemir is no fool", Abdarakos said. "He knows that the Goths will incur the wrath of the Eastern Empire if they waged open war upon the Rugii, the allies of the Western Empire. That is the reason why he proposed the marriage between Gisa and Feva. Why send ten thousand warriors if one woman can achieve the same result?"

"Why did Flaccitheus not refuse the union?" I asked.

"Because he knows that the Rugii cannot stand against the Goths", Abdarakos said. "After the combined armies of the Rugii, Scirii, Heruli, Gepids and Suebi had tasted defeat at Bolia, he had no choice but to accept her as his daughter-in-law."

"She is a beautiful woman", I said.

"Even Hella, the dark one, can appear as a comely maiden", Kursik said. "The prettier, the more sinister."

"Is Unni not pretty?" I asked.

"There are exceptions to the rule", Kursik replied with a scowl, and kicked his horse to fall in beside Boarex, who rode ten paces ahead of us.

I found myself riding alongside my grandsire.

"How will you convince Theodemir of the Goths to refrain from invading the West?" I asked.

"I will threaten him", Abdarakos said.

"With war?" I asked.

The erilar issued a snicker through his grey beard. "Theodemir of the Goths does not fear the armies of the Heruli and the Rugii", he said. "He is a hard bastard, who, like me, fought under the banner of the great khan."

"How will you threaten him then?"

"I have something that he fears more than all the armies of the realm of men combined", Abdarakos said, and steered his mare closer. "He fears you, Ragnar, more than death itself."

"Me?" I asked, waiting for the laughter that would show that the erilar jested. Yet, it did not come.

"He believes that you are his son – the legitimate heir to the throne", my grandsire said. "If the Goth warriors knew the truth, it would rip the tribe apart."

"Am I his son?" I asked.

Abdarakos did not meet my gaze. "It matters not. What matters is that Theodemir knows that his warriors will rather follow a man with iron in his veins - a man the likes of you, Ragnar. They

176

will reject Theoderic, the boy who had been raised as a pampered noble in the halls of the imperial palace in the City of Constantine."

"Theodemir will kill us all", I said.

"He will not", Abdarakos said, "because he will wish to keep your existence a secret from Theoderic, who believes that he is the only legitimate heir."

I allowed my thoughts to drift back to the time after the battle of Bolia when I was captured by the Goths. "Theodemir told me that it was prophesied that his son would become the father of a great nation", I said. "Why would he then fear my existence?"

Again, Abdarakos snickered. "Do you think that that prophecy was meant for Theoderic?" he asked.

Then it dawned on me – the words could have been meant for me.

My realisation did not go unnoticed. "Theodemir has figured that one out as well", the erilar said.

Chapter 22 – Ambush

The Ostrogoth camp near Vindobona, Pannonia Prima, province of the East Roman Empire.

(Present day Vienna, Austria)

"Lord", Abdarakos said, and inclined his head to the king of the Ostrogoths.

"Your presence is unexpected, Lord Abdarakos", Theodemir replied, but appeared less than surprised. "I heard a rumour that Rodolph, your king, had expelled you from his lands."

For some reason or other, maybe because of the way it was said, his words created the impression that it was more than a rumour – that he had firsthand knowledge of the event.

Abdarakos ignored the jibe. "This is my grandson, Ragnar", he said, and laid a hand upon my shoulder. "But I understand that you have already made his acquaintance."

The erilar's words visibly unsettled King Theodemir, who for a brief moment wore the look of a trapped animal. But he gathered himself and gestured for a young man, who was of an age with me, to step forward. "Prince Theoderic, my heir, has just returned from his successful campaign against the Sarmatian king, Babai."

Abdarakos acknowledged the young prince with a bow of his head. "It is a blessing from the gods when there is only one heir to the throne. A unified tribe is as strong as iron."

The prince had no idea of the veiled threat contained in the words of Abdarakos and inclined his head in acceptance of the compliment. "Thank you, lord", he replied. "God is good indeed."

Theodemir grimaced in reply, "Come, General Abdarakos. Join me, and we will share a horn of mead in private to speak about times long gone, when we fought side by side under the banner of the great khan."

* * *

"Theodemir accepted my terms", Abdarakos said. "And he invited us to a feast."

"Is it wise to remain in the Goth camp?" I asked.

"Do you think me a fool?" Abdarakos growled. "It will give the Goth king time to plot our demise. We leave now."

"Will Theodemir be true to his word?" I asked.

"Theodemir is many things", Abdarakos said. "But an oathbreaker he is not. He will try to kill us to free him from his promise, but if I remain alive, he will keep his word."

We galloped along a dirt track through a sea of tents, wagons and lean-to huts. It was clear that the Goths had fallen on hard times. Their garments were tattered and many of the toddlers and oldsters emaciated. Under the banner of Attila, the Goths had taken to the way of the horse, but I noticed few mounts – many warriors having traded their greatest asset for a few days of going to bed with a full stomach.

When we left the confines of the sprawling camp, we allowed the horses free rein and thundered north along the Roman road, heading towards Noricum.

"They will soon realise that we have fled", Ferderuchus said. "We must cross into Rugiland as soon as we can. There is a ferry at the town of Commagenis, twenty miles to the west."

We spoke little, knowing the importance of placing as many miles as possible between us and our pursuers. Not long after, we thundered past the blackened ruins of a small town. "Asturis", Ferderuchus said, indicating the burnt-out remains. "Handiwork of the Goths. Years ago, Severinus warned the elders of the town

180

of its imminent destruction, but they failed to heed the holy man's warning."

Outside Asturis the road turned west and the overgrown, long-abandoned fields gave way to woodlands. The trees encroached upon the road, until a thick forest of beech and oak dimmed out the light of the sun. We continued along the dilapidated cobbled road until we burst from the gloom near the walls of Commagenis. Somewhere in the woods we had crossed the unmarked border into Roman Noricum.

We bypassed the walls of the town, the Roman sentries watching us from the battlements atop the closed gate. Ferderuchus led us to the bank of the river where a ferry was anchored forty paces offshore.

Although the ferryman was dressed as a Roman, Ferderuchus hailed him in the tongue of the Germani, and received an answer in kind. Within moments the crew poled the ferry, which must have been a Roman barge from bygone times, closer to the bank.

"M'lord", the ferryman said and bowed low. "Do you wish to cross, m'lord?"

Ferderuchus did not answer, but opened his palm, revealing three silvers. At once, without being instructed, the three crewmen poled the barge to the water's edge. I assumed they were the kin of the ferryman, as they all had the same ratty look about them.

The prince closed his fist as soon as the ferryman stretched out his hand. "When we get to the other side", he said.

One of the men started to complain, "But dada …"

"Shut your trap, boy", the ferryman sneered, "or I will do if for you."

He turned to Ferderuchus, wearing a false, gap-toothed smile. "Apologies, m'lord prince. Forgive m'boy. He's got very little behind his eyes, lord. Poor thing takes after his mother. God bless her soul."

While we glided across the water, my grandsire asked Ferderuchus, "How come the ferryman knows you?"

"He does not", Ferderuchus replied and patted the rich embroidery on the breast of his woollen tunic. "It is not hard to guess, though."

When we had disembarked on the far bank, the prince handed three silver coins to the drooling ferryman. Then he passed him a fourth. "This is to buy your silence."

"My lips are sealed, m'lord", he called while the barge drifted away from the bank.

"He has been forewarned and will sell us out", the erilar said, and nodded to Kursik and Boarex who had both strung their bows. Five heartbeats later the lifeless bodies of the ferryman and his sons drifted downstream, outpacing the barge.

Kursik dragged the ferryman's corpse from the shallows, cut the purse, and handed it to Abdarakos who emptied it in his hand. Amongst the coppers were five gold solidi bearing the image of Leo the Thracian.

"The East Romans pay their tribute to the Goths in gold. Theodemir has already paid him for his treachery", Abdarakos growled, spat in the dust, and kicked his horse to a canter.

But Abdarakos was wrong – in part, anyway. Although it was the Goths who had been planning our demise, it was not Theodemir.

* * *

Although we had crossed the Danube and entered the domain of Flaccitheus, we were still in the borderlands. Bands of Ostrogoths, Slavs and other brigands regularly infiltrated the area to raid the farms and settlements of the Rugii.

I rode at the rear of the column, beside Kursik.

183

"We are being followed", he said in the tongue of the Huns.

"How do you know?" I asked.

"I know", he replied.

I had come to appreciate the animal-like senses of my Hun friend.

"When the track passes through the woods, we will stage an ambush", I replied.

In response to my words the Hun fiddled with a leather pouch, choosing the appropriate bowstring befitting the occasion. He closed his fist around his preferred string and retied the little sealskin bag to his belt. "Hemp", he stated and wiped the drizzle from his brow. "Sinew will break in this weather."

The Romans knew the art of constructing well-drained, straight stone roads, but Rugiland had never been under their dominion. In times of old the Quadi were the masters of the land, but they had long before been crushed by the armies of the great khan. Flaccitheus had simply taken advantage of the void after the death of Attila, and seized the lordless lands. For this reason, the road we travelled was little more than a muddy cart path meandering past small peasant fields and the occasional green meadow. But, predominantly, the greenway cut a path through the ancient forest of hornbeam, oak, fir and beech.

184

More than a mile farther the track descended into a forested valley. We carefully negotiated the particularly slippery slope, made muddy and treacherous by the interminable drizzle.

I nodded to Kursik and we steered our horses from the path, which had become a stream of sorts, fed by rivulets from the surrounding greenwood.

Abdarakos, who rode ahead of us, somehow noticed. I pointed to my eyes and my bow, indicating our intention. The erilar held my gaze for three heartbeats, then issued a small nod of approval.

We watched from the shadows as three mounted warriors appeared at the top of the descent. Kursik nocked an arrow to the string, but kept his horn bow underneath his sealskin cloak. The Hun indicated the trailing warrior, then gestured towards my bow. I nodded.

The threesome picked their way down the slope. When they drew level with us, Kursik raised his bow. The broad-headed hunting arrow slammed into the temple of the lead warrior, throwing him from the saddle. I played it safe and my armour-piercing arrow easily split the chainmail protecting the chest of the trailing rider. The middle rider spurred his horse, which lost its footing as a result. He careened over the neck of the stumbling animal and collided with the trunk of a hornbeam. Moments later, with a sickening crunch, the horse landed heavily on top of the prone warrior.

Kursik unstrung his pride and joy and stowed it in a watertight pouch.

"Poor animal", I heard the Hun mumble as he slipped his razor-sharp dagger from its sheath and strolled towards the injured man.

Chapter 23 – Heathens

The warrior I had hit in the chest was dead, as was the one struck by Kursik's arrow.

I found the Hun kneeling beside the man who was crushed by his own horse.

"Gisa, Vidimir's daughter, sent a message to her father", Kursik said while he meticulously wiped the bright blood from his blade. "We have to make haste", he added. "A large warband has been sent to ambush the erilar."

"Did he say why?" I asked.

"They need bait to lure King Flaccitheus into a trap", the Hun said. "With Flaccitheus dead, Feva will succeed to the throne, and then Gisa will hold the power in her hands. She will allow her father, Vidimir, and his Goths to settle in the lands of the Rugii."

"You learned much", I said, surprised at the wealth of information the Hun was able to extract from the dying man.

"Once they start talking, only a blade will silence them", the Hun replied and issued a wolflike grin.

We mounted and rode as swiftly as possible in an attempt to warn our friends of the Goth ambush.

Two miles farther the road winded up a hill and exited the forest into a clearing. We could still hear the thunder of hooves of the retreating Goths.

At the side of the path we found the body of Asbadus facedown in the mud, a Gothic lasso pulled tight around his neck, and a spearhead with a severed haft lodged in his leg. The bloodstained soil which surrounded his corpse bore witness to the fact that he had sold his life dearly. His magnificent axe had no doubt been taken as spoils.

I vaulted from my horse, turned Asbadus onto his back, and gently wiped the dirt from his bearded face. Cradling his head in my hands, I cut the lasso from his neck, revealing a bloody, purple welt. A terrible sadness rose from within and I pressed my forehead onto the big Isaurian's chest.

Suddenly Asbadus drew breath with a mighty gasp and both his hands clutched at the place that the braided lasso had occupied moments before.

I stumbled backwards in shock, nearly ending up in the mud. When I had regained my composure, I noticed that Asbadus was still staring at me with wide eyes. "Where is my axe?" he croaked, tried to rise, and crumpled to the ground, unconscious.

Just then a deep moan emanated from within the underbrush at the side of the clearing. Kursik took his battle-axe in his hand, swung from the saddle, and gestured for me to join him.

We found Boarex lying on his back, moaning. The Hun was bleeding profusely from a deep cut to his shoulder where a blade had split his mail.

One at a time we carried the wounded men into the greenwood, well away from the track. Kursik used dry tinder, which he always kept tied to his saddle, to light a fire. I filled my cooking pot from a nearby stream and suspended it above the flames. Kursik cut his woollen cloak into strips and immersed it in the boiling water.

We removed Boarex's armour, cleaned his wound with vinegar, and sealed it with honey.

Removing the spear from Asbadus's leg proved a challenge, but eventually we succeeded, although he lost much blood. We wrapped the wound tightly in an attempt to stanch the bleeding.

"Look after our friends for a while", Kursik said when we were done. He swung up into the saddle, his dagger in his fist. "I will be back soon."

189

* * *

Kursik could not have been gone for more than two hours, but it felt like an eternity. He moved with such stealth that I failed to notice his return until his horse whinnied ten paces from where I sat in vigilance, between Asbadus and Boarex.

Streaks of red dripped from the flanks of his horse and I spied three fresh scalps adorning his saddle.

The Hun shrugged in answer to my enquiring stare. "It is going out of fashion, I know. But I thought I would make an exception for these Goths."

His gaze shifted to the two wounded men in turn.

"They still breathe", I said and he issued a curt nod in reply.

"The erilar lives", Kursik said. "The Goths are making camp on a hillock north of here. There are at least a hundred of them."

"Flaccitheus has many more men to call on", I replied.

Again, the Hun nodded. "That is why I scouted farther", he said. "Two larger warbands are camped less than a mile from the first. They are setting up a trap – a triple ambush. The warriors that I saw were no rabble, they are hard men – well-armed and clad in chain and scale."

"They are the ringmen of a king", I guessed. "Did you spy a noble amongst them?"

"I saw a greybeard chieftain mounted on a splendid grey stallion", he said and handed me a piece of dried deer meat. "It will be the brother of Theodemir, the one who is called Vidimir."

"We have no choice but to take Boarex and Asbadus to the Rugii stronghold", I said between mouthfuls. "Else they will die."

Once we had made the injured men as comfortable as we could, we took care of the horses and spread our furs on the damp soil.

"I will wake you to take the second watch", the Hun said and walked into the shadows.

I pulled a fur over my tired body and drifted off to sleep.

The following morning, when it was light enough to travel, Kursik and I set off, each of us riding double with a wounded comrade. The two injured men drifted in and out of consciousness and would have fallen from the saddle had we not tied them to us with leather straps.

Three hours after dark, we eventually found ourselves before the gate of the stronghold of Flaccitheus. Kursik and I were dead tired, our horses close to collapse and, for a full watch, we had not checked whether our wounded friends still drew breath, for fear that they had already expired from loss of blood.

Arriving at the hall of the king we found Atakam outside, as if he had been expecting us.

Flaccitheus stormed from the door, surrounded by his hearthmen. "Where is my son?" the old king asked as his men helped carry our wounded friends into the hall.

"He lives, lord", I said.

The king nodded and gestured for us to follow him. "Come", he said and bade us to enter. "You can tell all while you slake your thirst."

While we told our tale and Atakam tended to our friends, Severinus arrived.

"The Lord came to me in a dream", he said. "Take heed, do not pursue the Goths, Lord King. If you follow, you will be slain. Place your trust in the Lord."

The holy man approached the king and whispered into his ear, loud enough for me to hear, "The heathens will wish to go – allow them."

I retired to the furs with a stomach filled with pottage and ale, knowing that Boarex and Asbadus were in good hands. If Atakam and the healers of the king could not bring them back to health, then it was the will of the gods.

On the morrow Atakam woke us at sunrise.

He handed us four aleskins and a leather pouch filled with smoked pork, boiled eggs and cheese. "Eat in the saddle", he said. "Abdarakos needs you."

"Wat can we do against hundreds of Goths?" I asked in desperation.

"I suggest you ask the gods", the shaman said, and slapped the rump of my horse.

Chapter 24 – Vidimir

While I waited for the Hun to scout out the Goth camp, I prayed to the gods, like Atakam had suggested.

I knew that Vidimir's men would have found the bodies of the three warriors who had fallen to our arrows. They would know that someone had escaped their ambush, and count on them to go straight to the Rugii king. Flaccitheus was known as a man of action, so Vidimir would expect him to immediately ride to the aid of his son.

When Kursik eventually returned, he shook his head, lips pursed. "There are many more of them than I initially thought", he said. "There must be close to eight hundred, although most of them are watching the road in ambush."

"The erilar and our friends?" I asked.

"They are kept in the centre of the camp", he said. "Many of the elite Goth warriors guard the tent. If we attempt to free the erilar, we must be prepared to die."

"That is why we will not try to free Abdarakos", I said as a plan took shape in my mind.

* * *

I cleared the leaves from the forest floor with my boots, revealing dark, damp soil. The disturbed earth filled my nostrils with a rich, musty aroma. For a heartbeat I thought that maybe Theodemir the Goth was my father because I, too, experienced the allure of the soil. Had the Goths not farmed the land for aeons?

"I find the smell of dirt revolting", the Hun growled, and spat onto the leaves, his actions strengthening my suspicions. "It is the smell of death."

I ignored his words and drew a large circle in the muck. "This is the camp of the Goths", I said, and fashioned another smaller circle at the centre of the camp. "Abdarakos is kept here."

Kursik grunted his agreement.

"Where is the tent of Vidimir?" I asked.

Kursik held out his hand for the sharpened stick and proceeded to scratch a crooked line to one side of the larger circle. "Their camp abuts a stream, which flows downhill, from here to here", he said, indicating the direction.

"The king does not wish to bathe in water soiled by the piss of his warriors", he said and rammed the stick into the earth, close to the perimeter of the circle. "Many sentries patrol the woods near to where the king has his tent."

"We will wait until dark", I said, and explained my intention to the Hun, who listened in silent amusement.

When I was through, he regarded me with raised eyebrows. "I will make my peace with the sky-father while we wait for the sun to set", he said. "I suggest you do the same."

Having followed my friend's advice, we set out at twilight. We wore no armour – not yet anyway. The thick carpet of leaves helped to mask any sound as we slowly and silently made our way towards the camp of the Goths. Half a mile from our destination we tied our mounts to a tree and proceeded on foot. The gods had gifted Kursik with the senses of a feral beast, and I allowed him to lead the way.

First I smelled the aroma of grilling meat, carried our way on the back of a thin breeze. Then I heard the telltale sounds of warriors communing around cooking fires. When I stopped to listen, I could make out the faraway sound of a bubbling brook. Suddenly Kursik went to ground. I followed suit and crouched behind the trunk of a large oak. I waited a hundred heartbeats, drew my dagger, and crept closer to where I had last seen my friend. I found him crouching beside the corpse of a Goth sentry which he had dragged into the cover of a clump of ferns. He indicated that I should assist him to remove the armour. There was little blood – the Hun's dagger still embedded up to the hilt in the eye socket of his victim.

Kursik assisted me to don the clothes and armour of the sentry, which, although dirty, was a reasonable fit. When I had strapped on the helmet, the Hun studied me for a while and nodded his approval.

Three more sentries died at the hands of the Hun before we reached the stream. I patted Kursik on the back, drew a deep breath, and waded through the shallow water, slowly counting to a hundred.

When I reached ninety, Kursik released his first shaft. Fortuna rewarded his efforts, and I heard a warrior scream in pain as his arrow found flesh. The Hun shot his arrows high up into the night sky so that they fell near the centre of the camp at a very steep angle, which made it almost impossible to determine where they originated from.

The time spent under the yoke of the Hun had made the Goths ethnically diverse, and none suspected anything as I shouted the alarm in my best Goth, even if my words carried a slight accent.

"The prisoners are escaping! The Rugii are attacking the camp! The prisoners are escaping!"

What followed can best be described as utter chaos. Kursik continued to pour arrows into the midst of the Goth camp while I approached the tent of the king at a run, axe in hand.

"We are under attack from the Rugii", I shouted to the hulking champion guarding the entrance to the tent. For a heartbeat his eyes left mine to take in the chaos behind me. In that moment I lashed out and the haft of my bearded axe struck him on the side of the helmet. He stumbled to the side and I hit him again, this time with the blunt end of the head, and he crumpled to the ground.

I knew that I had only a moment to cover my tracks. I half-lifted the unconscious warrior onto my shoulder and stormed through the doorway, pushing the embroidered felt flap aside with his body, which I held before me like a shield.

In the dimly-lit interior, another guard, who had no doubt drawn his sword when the raucous started, lashed out with his blade, which embedded in the back of the man I carried. I did not stop, and rushed the second guard who was frantically trying to free his blade. But he tripped on a thick fur, which I strangely recall to be that of a black fox, and fell backwards, striking his helmetless head against a cast iron brazier.

198

Five paces away, a heavyset greybeard watched the happenings with an expression best described as horrified fascination.

"Have you come to kill me?" he asked.

"No lord", I said, and took a step closer.

He slashed at me with a dagger that he had concealed behind his back. But I was young and fast as a viper. I hit his wrist with the haft of my axe and winded him with a blow to his stomach. Vidimir doubled over. The haft of my axe came around and struck him against the temple.

I cut through the back of the tent with the blade of my axe, heaved the unconscious king onto my shoulder, and ran into the darkness as fast as my legs could carry me.

* * *

An hour later Kursik helped me lift Vidimir from the back of my horse and lay him down on the furs.

"I think he's dead", Kursik said.

"It can't be", I replied, and rushed to the king to search for any sign of life, but there was none.

"By the gods", I said. "I've ruined it."

Kursik grunted his agreement.

"We will exchange him for Abdarakos and our friends", I said.

"Exchange a dead king?" Kursik mused.

"They don't know that he is dead", I said.

Kursik grinned in reply.

* * *

Vidimir, son of Vidimir, paced around the tent of his father.

My hands were tied behind my back while a hulking Goth, who stood behind me, held a dagger to my throat.

"Leave us", Vidimir said, addressing the guard.

"Lord", the guard objected, but Vidimir dismissed him with a wave of his hand.

"You wish for your grandsire, Lord Abdarakos's return?" he asked when we were alone.

"Yes lord", I replied. "I will return your father in exchange for their lives."

"No", he said, and took a heavy purse from a chest in the corner of the tent and showed me that it contained gold. "You will cut his throat."

I must have smiled as relief flooded over me.

The Goth lord misread my expression, assuming that I relished the prospect of ridding the world of Vidimir. "Make it as painful as you wish, heathen", he said. "Just make sure that he does not return."

"Take the gold and go", he added and cut away my bonds. "Tomorrow at sunrise I will release your kin. In return I wish for the head of the king."

"Do as you are told and you will earn another purse of gold!" he shouted as I exited the tent.

Chapter 25 – Exchange

The prince rode towards us, mounted on a magnificent grey stallion. I could not help but wonder whether the horse belonged to his father. His oathsworn remained a hundred paces distant, holding the reins of Abdarakos and his entourage's mounts.

"Show me the head", he said when he reined in, "then your kin will be released."

"A man who wishes for the head of his father cannot be trusted", I said. "You will murder me as soon as you know that I have killed King Vidimir. Release them or I will return your father to you in good health. When I told him about our conversation, he seemed eager to speak with you."

Young Vidimir bristled at my words, but, at the same time, appeared concerned that I might do what I had threatened to do. He issued a curt nod of surrender and waved his arm – no doubt the prearranged signal for the prisoners to be released.

Apart from the expected bruises and scratches, Abdarakos and my friends appeared unscathed. They were mounted on the same horses they rode when they were captured, which clearly indicated to me that young Vidimir wished that I, too, should uphold my end of the bargain.

Abdarakos reined in beside me and I noticed a look in his eye I had never seen before. He said naught, just nodded, but the gesture conveyed more than a thousand words.

"I know, grandfather", I whispered in the tongue of the Heruli. "Be ready."

Ten paces from me, Vidimir's horse, like its master, was getting restless.

I raised my hand and Kursik materialised from the mogshade at the side of the path. The Hun presented a leather pouch to the prince, who peered inside.

"Did he suffer?" he snarled when he recognised who the head had belonged to.

"Yes", I lied, which clearly pleased him.

"You have earned your gold", he said. "Wait while I signal for my guards to deliver it."

Kursik moved his mount in beside mine and whispered, "A large number of Goths are making their way towards the road."

I disregarded the empty promise of the prince, abruptly turned the head of my horse towards the north, and kicked it to a canter.

It did not take long to realise that the Goths were pursuing us. A hundred riders, the best of Vidimir's men, thundered after us on the muddy track.

"What is your plan?" Abdarakos asked as his horse drew abreast of mine.

"I suggest we do not allow them to catch us", I said, having not thought that far ahead.

"It is a good plan", the erilar said. "For they will kill us when they do."

It was a strange statement, but by way of explanation, Abdarakos gestured to a deep cut on his horse's rump. The wound had opened with the heavy riding. "Most of our horses carry wounds", he said. "Vidimir knows it."

"We leave no one behind", I said. "When the first horse goes lame, we make a stand."

Abdarakos nodded his approval. "We will all arrive at Ulgin's mead hall together", he said. "Remember, the first to fall gets the best seat, nearest to the barrels."

Our horses lasted longer than we thought. With five miles to go to the hall of Flaccitheus, Beremud's horse began to falter.

About halfway along a long straight stretch of the path, the big Goth reined in. "The animal is dead on its hooves", he said, and shook his bearded head with lips pursed. "Leave me, I will stall them", he added and drew his great sword.

"You are too fat for the poor animal", Kursik said in reply. Then the Hun vaulted from his horse and joined Beremud in the centre of the track, testing the draw of his horn bow with five arrows in his fist.

Trokondas, Abdarakos and I joined our two comrades, our weapons ready. The two princes, Ottoghar and Ferderuchus, stood shoulder to shoulder, their blades at the ready.

The pursuing Goths were at least four hundred paces away when Kursik whispered, "There are men in the woods", he said.

"They must have anticipated our flight", I said. "But it matters not. Seven against a hundred leaves the same result as seven against two hundred."

While I waited for the inevitable I felt no fear, but rather sorrow and regret. I would never be able to say goodbye to Unni, and none would survive to tell her the tale of our demise.

"Here they come", Abdarakos said, and drew his mighty blade.

Kursik and I had arrows nocked while Trokondas weighted his bearded axe in his fist.

The horsemen, knowing that they had caught their prey, reined in.

"Hold your arrows", Abdarakos said. "The Goth pup wants to gloat."

The column of Goths, led by the young Vidimir, trotted towards us, then slowed down to a walk. The prince came to a halt a few paces from us, flanked by his heavily armoured, hulking guards.

Moments later, Goths armed with iron-tipped spears emerged from the greenwood, and like a grim guard of honour, lined up on both sides of the path, their spears levelled.

Vidimir leered at us, no doubt enjoying the moment. "And here we are", he said, shaking his head in mock amusement. "Do not be concerned, you will not suffer. For years to come, my people will talk about my benevolence – the king who executed the murderers of his father without the need for cruelty. I suggest …"

But Vidimir got no further. Two hundred paces up the road, from around a bend, a lone horseman appeared. He seemed to be in no hurry and walked his horse down the track at a lazy, neverminded gait.

All attention was focused on the unfortunate stranger, who, by some curse of the gods, was walking into what would soon be a slaughter ground. It was clear that the lone rider was a warrior. He wore a magnificent gilded helmet, inlaid with silver and edged with chain. His whole body was protected by scale and plate, and at his hip hung a longsword.

Vidimir frowned. "Who is that fool?" he spat, but the aloofness of the approaching stranger eroded the confidence conveyed in the prince's words, and made it sound like the whining of a petulant child.

When the rider was close enough, I realised that he was whistling a jolly tune, a tune I had heard many a time. Involuntarily I smiled.

The great boat lord removed his boar-crested helmet with both hands. "I am Mourdagos, overlord of the Western Heruli", he said, addressing Vidimir. "Why do you face off against my kin with your blades bared?" the big man growled.

"The more the merrier", Vidimir said, eager to get the killing done.

He was about to mouth the order when Mourdagos raised an open palm. "I have travelled far to answer the call of my kin. Four thousand of my best men, wolf-warriors all, wait in the shadows", he said, and gestured to the dark woods.

The boat lord folded his oaken arms across his chest.

By then, Vidimir's eyes were darting between the greenwood and Mourdagos, trying to decide whether the Heruli chieftain was bluffing.

"Leave", Mourdagos sneered. "I have no quarrel with the Goths. Do not give me a reason to slay you all."

Vidimir, having come to a decision, pointed his sword at Mourdagos. "Put a spear through his heart", he commanded the hulking warrior at his right.

The man hefted his blade, but with a woosh, a Hun arrow slammed into the Goth's chest, throwing the corpse from the saddle.

"Hold", Mourdagos thundered in a booming voice - the power of the big man's will keeping the standoff from turning into a bloodbath. The boat lord nudged his mount forward, until only a handspan separated his face from Vidimir's perspiring brow.

"Leave... or die", he growled.

Chapter 26 – Army

When the last of Vidimir's Goths had disappeared around a far bend in the path, Abdarakos turned in the saddle to face Mourdagos.

"Your army moved as swiftly as the wind", the erilar said.

Before the big man could offer a reply, the shaman came limping from the mogshade, a Hun bow in his fist.

"My warriors are still days away", Mourdagos said. "But it appears that Atakam is all I need to put the fear of the gods into the Goths", he added with a smirk.

"Why did you come, then?" Abdarakos asked, sensing that there was a reason for the presence of his brother-in-law.

Mourdagos's face turned serious. "My informers tell me that the Longobardi are gathering their allies. There is no time to waste, we must make haste to the lands of the Heruli before it is too late."

"That we will, brother", he said. "But first I have business with Flaccitheus of the Rugii."

"Business?" he asked.

"I wish to ask a favour", the erilar said.

"Will Flaccitheus grant it?" he said.

"He already has", Abdarakos replied and turned his horse towards the north.

* * *

"Three thousand warriors?" King Flaccitheus said. "What you ask is nearly impossible."

"We will be fools to leave these lands devoid of spears", Feva echoed his father, but all knew that he spoke the words of Gisa.

Ferderuchus intervened on behalf of the erilar. "Lord Abdarakos convinced Theodemir to turn his gaze to the East, and he freed us from the clutches of Vidimir. That, Father, is impossible", he said. "What he asks of us in return is not impossible, it is merely difficult."

Flaccitheus hung his head in shame. "You are right, son", he said. "Forgive me erilar. I will summon my best warriors from the four corners of the land. Ferderuchus will lead them north in five days' time."

Just then the holy man, Severinus, entered the hall. He inclined his head to us. "Lords", he said. "I have come to wish you farewell. I am returning south, to Noricum, to tend to my flock. They will need me in the dark days to come."

Surprisingly, Atakam, of all people, answered. "Two of our men will escort you south, priest", he said.

"I do not have gold to reward them with", Severinus said. "The Lord will protect me."

"You have ink and parchment?" Atakam asked.

Severinus nodded.

"All they will require is a letter of safe passage", the shaman said. "Who will dare risk the wrath of your Lord by defying the will of his priest?"

"I will do as you ask, heathen", Severinus replied. "I leave at first light."

We were all baffled by the strange conversation between the holy men, but knew that Atakam would reveal his intentions when it suited him.

Later that evening when we shared ale around the hearth, the shaman enlightened us. "The Longobardi is not to be underestimated", he said. "For generations they have made their way south along the Amber Road, clearing a bloody route with spear and sword. Many tribes have tried to stop their inexorable progress, but against the odds, the Longobardi have prevailed."

"They are yet to face the Heruli", Abdarakos growled.

"You, Abdarakos, must be the one who brings the Longobardi to heel", Atakam said. "But realise this – we are all playthings in the hands of the gods. Rome, the greatest empire of all time, is crumbling. One day the Longobardi, the Heruli and the Goths, like the Huns, will be but a distant memory. Nothing lasts forever."

"Speak plainly, shaman", Abdarakos said. "I do not understand your riddles."

"Although you will need all the help you can get, the fate of some of us lie elsewhere", he said. "It is the will of the gods."

Atakam pointed a bony finger at Trokondas and Asbadus, who sat beside me. "Follow the destiny that the gods have ordained", he said. "Do not allow your sense of obligation to distract you from your path."

The shaman held up a hand to stall Trokondas's response. "The time has come for you to travel south with Father Severinus and return to the Great City in the East."

Trokondas said naught for a hundred heartbeats, staring into the fire. Then he issued a deep sigh. "You are right, shaman", he said. "I feel it in my heart, there is no denying it. Tomorrow morning, Asbadus and I will travel south with the holy man."

When everyone else had retired to their furs, Trokondas and I remained beside the hearth.

"I do not know if I will ever see you again, Ragnar", he said. "But if you find yourself without friends, look to the East because while I still draw breath I will come to your aid."

"If you tire of the backstabbing in the Great City you are welcome at my hearth", I replied.

* * *

"My men are camped five miles south of the main Heruli camp", Prince Ottoghar said and pointed at the place which I used to call home.

Over the past few years Ottoghar had become a warlord in his own right. It is true that his men fought for the Western Empire and that they were paid in Roman gold, but there was no doubt

213

where their loyalties lay - not with Rome, but with the charismatic Scirii prince.

Two thousand Scirii spearmen, the remnants of his own people, constituted the core of his force. A thousand mounted Suebian swordsmen and a thousand mounted Heruli, of which more than a few were Huns, formed the cavalry. Another thousand heavy infantry were a mix of Franks, Burgundians, Visigoths, Britons, Gepids and Thuringians – all men who had left their hearths, either by fate or by choice, to seek their fortunes in far lands. There were even a few powerfully built, squat men, no doubt Romans whose proud forebears had conquered the world.

Prince Ottoghar rode abreast of Abdarakos. Boarex, Kursik and I followed close behind with Atakam and the big Goth, Beremud, bringing up the rear.

I heard the approach of horsemen, and Ottoghar reined in. From around a bend in the path a group of twenty riders appeared. They, too, went from a canter to a slow trot, reining in ten paces from us.

The lead horseman removed his full face helmet. I recognised his clean-shaven face immediately. It was Julius, one of the ringmen of Ottoghar.

Julius inclined his head to the prince. "We have been expecting you for some days now, lord", he said.

His eyes washed over the few men who accompanied his lord. Not able to hide the disappointment in his voice, he said, "I had hoped that you would have gathered more warriors, lord."

Ottoghar said naught about the thousands of Rugii and Boat Heruli who were soon to arrive. "Do not be concerned, Julius", he replied. "Every man you see here is worth a thousand warriors."

A frown settled on Julius's brow. It was clear that he had great difficulty making sense of Ottoghar's words.

"How many men would Rome trade to bring back your forefather, the great Julius Caesar? What is the worth of a man like the great khan, Attila?" Ottoghar asked.

Julius's gaze settled on Abdarakos, taking in the scarred visage of the erilar. "I believe I understand, lord", he said, then turned around to face his men. "We will escort our lord back to camp", he said, then pointed at a man sporting a Suebian topknot. "Ride ahead, tell the men that Tribune Flavius Odovaker has returned."

Chapter 27 - Rodolph

*__The Herulian camp on the Amber Road in the barbarian lands
north of Roman Noricum.__*

__(Present day Moravian Gate, Hranice, Czechia)__

Rodolph, the young, clean-shaven king of the Heruli, waited for
us in front of his opulent tent.

He wore a long-sleeved woollen tunic edged with black fur. The
red garment was thickly woven and elegantly embroidered with
swirling yellow patterns depicting a variety of wild animals and
ferns. A gold brooch, inlaid with green gemstones, secured the
grey wolfskin cloak draped around his shoulders. An ornate
longsword hung from a broad leather belt decorated with golden
plaques etched with runes. His deerskin breeches were tucked
into knee-length riding boots, dyed to match the colour of his
tunic.

Beside me, Abdarakos issued a low guttural growl, not unlike a
wolf ready to attack. "The gods help me for the sake of my
people", he muttered through clenched teeth, and reined in.

"Welcome, erilar", Rodolph said and extended his arms to his sides in a welcoming manner, his open palms facing us. "I am overjoyed that you have answered my call, although we have had our differences in the past."

My grandsire swung from the saddle. For a span of heartbeats he scrutinized the gathered nobles, who, in most cases, averted their eyes in shame. He exhaled heavily, walked towards Rodolph, and embraced him. Then he retreated a step.

"Now is the time for us to stand united", Abdarakos boomed for all to hear. He thrust his open hand in the air and made a show of slowly closing it until his knuckles showed white. "We must come together, like fingers on a hand." He then slammed his balled fist into his open palm. "And we will crush the Longobardi with a fist of iron."

Everyone assembled knew the reputation of the grizzled old warlord, whose words inspired confidence. All cheered in reply – all except Rodolph.

* * *

Abdarakos was not fool enough to remain in the den of the lion. Before the sun set, we returned to the camp of Ottoghar.

"We will travel north under a banner of truce to speak with King Aldihoc of the Longobardi", Abdarakos said, and took a swig from his ale horn.

"Do you believe that he will listen to reason?" Ottoghar asked.

"He will not", the erilar replied. "But word of my arrival will draw Heruli warriors to our banner – warriors who would not have fought beside Rodolph. For this, we need time."

"Ragnar and I will go", he said. "Atakam will accompany us. The Longobardi still revere the old gods."

"I will travel with you", Ottoghar said.

"No", Abdarakos replied. "You must stay here. There are matters of great importance that you have to attend to."

The Scirii prince frowned in reply, but the erilar took him by the arm and led him from the tent. "Come, I will tell you what needs to be done where no one can hear our words."

* * *

The following morning, Abdarakos, Atakam, Kursik and I set out towards Budorigum, the trading station on the western bank of the Oder. The Heruli still controlled the town, although the Longobardi's push south threatened to engulf the settlement.

"What did you speak to Prince Ottoghar about?" I asked.

"What do you think?" the erilar asked in return.

"It has to do with Rodolph", I guessed.

"He cannot be trusted", Abdarakos said. "Rodolph is no warrior. He tries to rule with the tongue rather than the sword. I am not so certain that he will not betray us."

"But he asked us to come to his aid", I said.

"I spoke with elders of the tribe today", the erilar replied with a sidelong glance. "They said that Rodolph has grown close to Prince Theoderic, the son of Theodemir. They are like brothers."

"Theoderic spent ten years in the City of Constantine", I replied, "where he was tutored by Aspar the Goth."

Abdarakos nodded. "That is the reason why we must be careful. I have told Ottoghar to ride east and intercept Mourdagos and his four thousand men. We will not commit all of my brother-in-law's men to the battle against the Longobardi. Two thousand will be kept as a reserve in case there is treachery afoot."

Later that afternoon we made camp on the western bank of the Oder. While a thick mutton and barley pottage simmered in a copper pot above the cooking fire, we shared a skin of mead.

Abdarakos rarely spoke of the time of the great khan, but after the second cup of mead, he did.

"Men believe that Attila was a monster", the erilar said. "That he subjugated one tribe after another and put to death those who refused to follow his banner."

"Is it not true?" Prince Ottoghar asked.

"Yes, it is true", Abdarakos replied with a wan smile. "The strongest is awarded the spoils - this has always been the law of the Sea of Grass. Warlords come and go, but not often do the gods send a man of the likes of Attila into this world."

"The power of his will was so strong that all succumbed to it without the need for words. To his enemies he was an abomination, but to his allies he was like a father. Once you had clutched the golden torque of the great khan and given your oath before the gods, he would lay down his life for you, like a father would."

"None of the chieftains followed the Huns – no, we all fought for Attila", he said, and wetted his throat. "But Attila's sons were not like the great man, and they understood little of the ways of their father. They foolishly believed that power and respect can be inherited."

"On that fateful day at the Nedao River when the tribes cast off the yoke of the Huns, the Goths stood idly by while thousands of the bravest of our people sacrificed themselves for freedom. None would have thought less of the Goths if they had stayed true to the sons of Attila. But rather than choose a side, they watched as we fought."

"But it did not work out as they had thought it would", Abdarakos sneered. "The tribes, as well as the Huns, despised them from that day onward. That is why I will never trust a Goth", he added, and spat to emphasize his words.

* * *

The following afternoon we arrived at Budorigum. The town was no longer the booming settlement I remembered. Only a handful of fur traders exchanged their wares on the large field that used to be a bustling market.

"The merchantmen have all heard the rumours of war", Abdarakos said. "The amber now makes its way south along the

Elbe and the Vistula. The fur traders are a more resilient breed, but soon they, too, will disappear."

The absence of the amber traders made it easy to arrange stabling for our horses. We left them at Budorigum and hired a river boat with a crew to row us upriver to the lands of Aldihoc.

I suspected the captain of the boat, a man with a long, grey-white beard, to be a Longobardi. He greedily accepted the handful of silvers from the hand of Abdarakos, but when the coin was safely in his purse, I often caught him studying us, his gaze shifting between the tribal tattoos adorning our cheeks, and the blades attached to our belts.

When evening came, the oldster sought out a clearing on the bank of the river. We made our own camp and cooking fire fifty paces away from where the greybeard and his six men had pitched their tents. When we had filled our bellies with pottage and ale, we retired to our furs.

I heard the unmistakable sound of a sword sliding from a sheath. "Sleep with your blades beside you", Abdarakos growled. "They will come to slit our throats in the middle hour of the night. Kursik, you will take the first watch."

I woke as a terrible scream split the silence. In the faint glow of the fire I saw a man, one of the rowers, stagger backwards, his chest carved open by the blade of Abdarakos's longsword. Another two rushed at a grinning Kursik who gripped a battle-axe in his right fist and a dagger in the left. The iron of his axe cleaved the skull of the first man, the second fell to the ground, gurgling, with a dagger embedded in his neck.

The man who came for me had more skill. I blocked the thrust of his longsword and crushed his head with the blunt end of my bearded axe. I noticed the last rower lying at Atakam's feet, trying to stanch the bleeding from a wound to his stomach.

The greybeard, who was watching from twenty paces away, fell to his knees. "Lord", he said. "They didn't listen to me, lord. They are scum. I am in your debt for killing them, lord."

Abdarakos strode toward the kneeling Longobardı and took the man's head with a single blow from his mighty blade.

"Now it is not necessary to set a watch", he said, curled up in his furs, and promptly fell asleep.

Chapter 28 – Aldihoc (June 473 AD)

The king of the Longobardi gestured for Abdarakos and me to take our seats on the lush furs spread around the hearth in the centre of his tent. Beside him sat his son, the heir apparent, Prince Godehoc.

"Rumour has it that you had gone north for good", Aldihoc said while slaves served us brimming horns of golden ale.

"Here I am", the erilar said and shrugged.

"We do not covet the lands of the Heruli", the king said. "We wish to go south to the lands of Rome. Noricum and Pannonia are ripe for the picking. Maybe even Italia itself."

I could not help but think of the wolves and the bear. Another wolf was salivating at the prospect of feasting on the flesh of the Western Empire. I was not fool enough to speak my mind, and wisely kept my counsel.

"Is that what you told the Scirii before you chased them from their lands?" Abdarakos asked. "No, King Aldihoc, we will not allow you passage through our lands. If you wish to claim Noricum and Pannonia for yourself, you will have to carve a path through the Heruli. We have paid for our lands with the blood of our warriors and will not give it away on a whim."

Godehoc could no longer control his rage. "Father", he growled, "these men had been under the yoke of the Huns for too long." He sniffed the air and then wrinkled his nose. "Not only do they reason like horses", he said, "they even smell like mares."

Abdarakos's hand went to the hilt of his sword. "Then march your warriors through the Amber Gate, prince", he said, "and we will scatter your bones in the meadows for the vermin to feast on."

The Longobardi king stood from his seat and placed himself between Abdarakos and Godehoc. "There will be no insulting of our guests", he said, addressing the prince. "Not under my roof."

"Forgive me, lord", Godehoc said, addressing the erilar, but the sneer remained on his lips.

Even though both Aldihoc and Abdarakos knew that there would be war, the Longobardi king still invited us to a feast held in our honour. That night we ate well and enjoyed good ale. Not once did we speak of war.

* * *

Three weeks later, having overrun Budorigum without any resistance, Aldihoc led the Longobardi horde through the Amber Gate, the ancient corridor to the south.

Abdarakos met them on the flat expanse between the Mountains of the Boar to the west, and the Oder to the east.

Ottoghar's two thousand heavy infantry deployed in the centre, in the front four ranks. The great khan had not used the Scirii as the core of his infantry without reason. The time spent fighting for Rome had moulded them into an even more formidable force. Their barbarian heritage meant that they were fierce fighters, but their time under the imperial standard had instilled in them an iron discipline. No longer did they do battle wearing a motley collection of armour. Roman gold had paid for knee-length chain mail jerkins, riveted full face helmets, iron greaves and laminated oval shields. Each warrior carried a thick-hafted, medium-length stabbing spear with a leaf-shaped blade, and two lighter barbed javelins. In addition, swords and daggers were strapped to their belts.

In the fourth and fifth ranks, the prince placed his thousand mixed barbarian infantry, kitted out similarly to the Scirii.

Three thousand Rugii foot, commanded by Ferderuchus, constituted the left flank. They were armed with dual purpose spears that could be used for throwing or thrusting. With their

226

left hands they wielded iron-bossed hexagonal shields. Depending upon their agility for survival, they wore boiled leather armour and skullcaps rather than heavy iron.

At the rear of the Rugii, in neat formation, stood Ottoghar's thousand mounted Heruli, who were armoured in scale and sported helmets in the Roman cavalry style. They carried oval shields and thin-hafted, ten-foot lances with armour-piercing iron tips. Quivers filled with light javelins were strapped to their saddles. The prince's mounted Suebian swordsmen, a thousand strong, were trained to support the Herulian lancers. Once the lancers broke the cohesion of an enemy shield wall, the swordsmen would pour into the gap, slicing the foe to pieces.

On the right flank, Abdarakos commanded Rodolph and Mourdagos's Heruli. Most, nearly four thousand, were light infantry armed with spears, javelins and battle-axes. They were attired in a motley collection of chain, scale and leather armour. At the rear of the Heruli, Abdarakos deployed a thousand mounted bowmen. They were mostly Huns, or the like, who had fought in Attila's ranks and chose to follow the erilar's banner after the demise of the khan's sons. Five hundred of the Heruli were heavily armoured noblemen who fought from horseback with sword, spear and shield. They were deployed at the rear of the Herulian foot, beside the Hun horsemen.

Altogether, nearly fourteen thousand warriors faced the Longobardi. Aldihoc's horde, that matched our numbers, were deployed in a single block with spear-wielding cavalry at each flank.

I sat in the saddle, behind Abdarakos, who was in overall command, stationed behind the Heruli infantry on the right. He had chosen the site because of the slight rise, which, especially from horseback, afforded us a panoramic view of the battlefield. Kursik, Beremud and I wore the armour of the excubitors. We would not fight in the ranks on the day, but guard the erilar.

When two hundred paces separated our front rank from the Longobardi, Abdarakos issued a command and the Huns released a single volley at the advancing horde. Although the enemy raised their shields, still a few shafts found flesh.

The erilar grinned when he heard the screams from the invaders' ranks. "We are welcoming them to the lands of the Heruli", he said.

Just then a ram's horn sounded from behind the advancing Longobardi. The warriors halted, and within heartbeats, arrayed into four giant wedge formations spread out over the thousand-pace frontage.

"We must stop the boar's snout", Abdarakos growled, and motioned to his signifier to issue the command. Moments later his signal was answered by Ottoghar's Roman buccina. The Scirii prince led his Herulian lancers around our left flank in a charge against the Longobardi wedges.

My grandsire gestured to the commander of the Hun cavalry to attend him. "Ride to the aid of Ottoghar", he said. "Aldihoc will send his mounted spearmen against our cavalry. Your task is to annihilate them."

The commander inclined his head, signalled to his men, and led the thousand horse archers into the fray around the edge of the right flank.

In answer to the Herulian lancers, the Longobardi horsemen launched their counter attack. They were armed with light javelins and stabbing spears – an ideal combination to counter the unwieldy lances. Before they could sweep the Heruli from the field, the Huns arrived, riding at breakneck speed. Wave after wave of Hun arrows slammed into the charging Longobardi, emptying hundreds of saddles as horses and riders went down in a tumble of limbs.

The wedge, or boar snout formation, is ideal for breaking through an enemy shield wall, but it is weak when subjected to attack by cavalry. The lancers first released their light javelins, then struck the disarrayed sides of the wedges with their ten-foot lances. The Longobardi suffered many casualties, forcing their advance to a grinding halt.

But the Longobardi also had archers who were stationed at their rear. Arrows arced over the heads of their infantry, forcing Abdarakos to order the withdrawal of the Scirii and the Huns.

While the last of the horsemen were still retreating, the erilar signalled for the entire army to advance.

A hundred heartbeats later, the front ranks came together with a sound reminding me of a large wave crashing onto a shingle beach. For long, the fighting raged. Frowning, the erilar studied the battle with intense concentration.

In the centre, the disciplined ranks of the heavily armoured Scirii were holding their own against the ferocious attack of the Longobardi. On the right, the Heruli beat back the onslaught of the foe. But on the left, the ranks of the Rugii were bending under the relentless pressure.

"Suebian cavalry to support the right", Abdarakos growled, and again the ram's horn echoed across the field of battle. A thousand mail-clad Germani spurred their mounts towards the edge of the left flank. But Aldihoc was no fool, and his mounted spearmen thundered to intercept the attack. A cloud of dust enshrouded the milling mass of cavalry as both sides tried to gain the upper hand.

Then disaster struck. The Longobardi's heavy infantry broke through the front ranks of Ferderuchus's men. The big, mailed warriors with the long beards spilled into the Rugii ranks, cutting the lightly armed warriors to pieces. I turned my mount to ride to their aid, but Abdarakos grabbed the reins of my horse and shook his head.

A great cheer emanated from the left, and for a moment I was sure it came from the victorious bearded warriors. But I was wrong. From the dust cloud on the right flank the remnants of the mounted spearmen of the Longobardi lay flat on their horses, fleeing for their lives. A short while later, neat ranks of Suebian swordsmen charged into the left flank of the enemy. Their reddened blades scythed from side to side, relentlessly cutting down the foe.

The Longobardi horn broke the spell. It must have signalled a withdrawal, as the foe disengaged and retreated ten steps. Although their blood was up, both sides were exhausted, therefore our men did not press their advantage.

"Signal orderly retreat", Abdarakos said.

'It is madness', I thought, but my grandsire divined my mind and fixed me with a stare before I could object.

"It is a stalemate", he growled, and in my heart I knew that he spoke true.

The two armies slowly backed away until eighty paces separated them.

"Come", Abdarakos said, and signalled for Kursik, Beremud and me to join him. "King Aldihoc will wish to talk."

Chapter 29 – Parley

Before we ventured out to parley, Abdarakos waved over the commander of the thousand Huns. "Hobble your horses and station half of your archers on each flank. Wait until the foe charges before you release."

Fighting on foot was something every Hun despised, but Abdarakos was not a man easily denied.

The Hun inclined his head. "Lord", he said, and left to give effect to the erilar's orders.

My grandsire waved for a messenger to approach. "Tell Prince Ottoghar to dismount his lancers as well as his Suebian swordsmen. They are to reinforce the Rugii line. I will give the signal for the men to sit and take repast, but be ready for treachery."

He waited until the messenger had repeated the message twice before he led us forward through the ranks.

Aldihoc, flanked by his son, Prince Godehoc, and two ringmen, slowly walked their horses towards our line. We met them in the middle.

"Your warriors fought well, erilar", Aldihoc said. "I suggest both our lines retreat another fifty paces to allow them time to eat and drink."

The erilar grunted his agreement and gestured for Beremud to deliver the message to Ottoghar. Similarly, one of Aldihoc's hearthmen returned to the Longobardi ranks.

We waited in silence until both armies had retreated the agreed distance. Before we could continue, a single rider detached from the Longobardi host and trotted towards our warriors. He rode with his arms extended to the side, open palms facing upwards.

Aldihoc shrugged, hinting that he had no knowledge of the unfolding events.

The hulking Longobardi rode up and down our line, taunting the warriors. "Is there no man who will face me in single combat?" he shouted. "Or are you an army of cowards?"

"This needs to end", Abdarakos growled in a whisper.

I felt a rage stir deep inside. Before I could subdue the beast, I heard myself shout, "I will face you, Longobardi pig!"

Two years before I had defeated the champion of the Usipetes, securing safe passage for the Longobardi through my actions. On that day, I had fought on foot, wielding my axe.

"You will be fighting from the back of a horse, boy", Aldihoc growled. "Your axe will not help you against the spear of Coccas."

"Are you willing to submit if Ragnar slays Coccas?" Abdarakos asked.

Aldihoc nodded in reply.

The erilar leaned in and pressed his forehead against mine. "Go kill him", he said. "The fools do not know that you were raised by a Hun."

I slipped my bearded axe from its holder and laid the haft across the saddle. Then I kicked my horse to a gallop, heading straight towards the Longobardi champion.

Coccas, who was two hundred paces away, turned the head of his horse to face me and urged it to a canter. He was tall and muscular, the bulging veins on his muscular forearms thick like cord. And he rode well, but for all his skill he was not a Hun.

I clamped my legs against the flanks of the horse and felt myself become one with the animal.

Coccas, now eighty paces away, raised his spear in an underhand grip, preparing for the killing blow.

I moved my horse to the right and took the haft of the axe in my left hand, indicating that I was left-handed. The Longobardi was a skilled warrior, and he knew that passing on my left would place him at a distinct disadvantage. He responded by pulling his horse to the left, countering my move.

I flicked my axe to my right hand and with my knees, nudged my horse to the left. Unbeknown to Coccas, it was a game played by Hun boys. They would charge at each other and attempt to outwit their opponent by passing him on the off-hand side.

At the crucial moment, when it was too late for Coccas to counter, I dropped my reins, and using only my knees, swerved to my right. The champion corrected his aim much quicker than I thought possible, and the spear left his hand like a bolt of thunder from the hand of a god. But the angle was less than perfect. I ducked instinctively. The powerful cast passed over my head, ripping scales from the armour on my back.

At that perfect moment when I was almost level with Coccas, and he was still unbalanced from the cast, I swung the axe backhanded, which is easier for a right-handed man. The Seric iron blade severed the links of his chain mail and cut deep into his side. He remained on his horse for forty heartbeats, then fell heavily from his saddle, his head striking the ground at an awkward angle.

236

A great cheer went up from the ranks of the Heruli, and, of course, the Longobardi charged.

"Well fought", the erilar said when I fell in beside him and Kursik, who were riding for the safety of our lines.

"It helped naught", I said and gestured towards the screaming Longobardi horde.

"Battles are won or lost in the hearts of warriors", Abdarakos growled. "They know that they have angered the gods with their treachery."

Before we passed through our front ranks, which were ready to repel the enemy, he paused to glance at the approaching foe. "They will expect defeat in every spear strike, every arrow, every blade that flashes – no man can fight when he knows the gods are not on his side."

The horde of bearded warriors struck our line just when we had returned to our position. Their remaining cavalry had dismounted and joined their infantry. Aldihoc was gambling all on one roll of the dice.

Although the pressure that the Longobardi exerted bent the line by forcing the Scirii back in the centre, Abdarakos smiled, seemingly unconcerned.

When the line was concave, the signifier issued a note on the horn of the war leader. The concave line had exposed the Longobardi's flanks to the dismounted Huns, who poured arrows into their unprotected ranks. It took only thirty volleys and double the number of heartbeats for the Longobardi to cast aside their weapons and flee.

Eager for the slaughter to come, the Herulian lines surged ahead, but Abdarakos's ram's horn held them in check.

The grizzled war leader turned to face me. "Plundering their camp will yield enough loot. Aldihoc will pay an annual tribute", he growled and indicated the fleeing Longobardi. "Dead men do not pay tribute."

* * *

When we arrived back at the Heruli camp, the king welcomed us with open arms.

"I have sent Longobardi prisoners back with a message for their king", Abdarakos told Rodolph. "He will come to you at daybreak tomorrow, else all the noble prisoners will die."

"You have done well, erilar", Rodolph replied. "Tonight we will feast in your honour."

"Forgive me, lord king", Abdarakos replied. "I am an old man and weary from the toil of the day. Allow me to rest this night and return on the morrow to accept your gratitude."

Abdarakos had won a great victory and the king knew that to refuse the erilar would reflect badly on him, so he reluctantly conceded.

When we arrived at Ottoghar's camp, the erilar retired to his tent. I walked to the nearby stream and washed the dirt, sweat and grime from my tired body. Afterwards I dressed in a clean tunic and lay down on the furs.

None other than Ottoghar himself came to my tent. "You are the hero of the day, Ragnar", he said, and judging by the slight slur in his speech, it was clear that he had already taken more than one horn of ale. "The men are calling your name. Come, together we will feast and give thanks to the gods for the victory."

Just then the felt flap was pushed aside and the old shaman ducked through the doorway. "The erilar wants you to attend him", he said to me. Ottoghar started to object, but Atakam silenced him with a raised palm. "You must come too, Lord Ottoghar."

239

"But we wish to honour the gods with a feast", the prince countered.

"The gods value obedience higher than debauchery", the old shaman replied, and gestured for us to follow him to the tent of Abdarakos.

We found the boat lord in the company of the erilar. Mourdagos, whose princely armour was spattered with gore and blood, raised his horn in a toast to my grandsire. "A warband of one thousand five hundred Goths walked into our ambush", he said. "Like you had predicted, brother."

"They were planning on attacking Ottoghar's camp this very night", Mourdagos added. "Once all were deep into their cups."

"How do you know this?" the Scirii prince asked.

"The Goth commander volunteered the information", the big man said and grinned through bloodstained teeth. Ottoghar knew better than to pursue the line of questioning.

"Have you heads?" the erilar asked.

"A few", Mourdagos confirmed.

"Get a man to deliver the trophies to King Rodolph", Abdarakos said. "Tell the king that we slew a band of Goths intruding on his lands. Mention to him that we are interrogating their commander and will report back tomorrow."

The flap of the tent parted and Kursik entered.

"Lord", he said, and bowed his head to the erilar. "You called for me."

"Come with me, Kursik", Abdarakos said. "I have a task for you."

* * *

The following morning Ottoghar, Abdarakos, Atakam and I arrived at Rodolph's tent before dawn. Strangely we were not summoned, but waited outside in the thick early-morning mist.

Soon there was a commotion and Aldihoc and his retinue of oathsworn arrived with an escort of Heruli warriors. We acknowledged the king's presence, but said little.

When the first rays of the sun appeared, Abdarakos pushed the flap aside and entered the tent, only to emerge moments later. "The king is not there", he announced.

Abdarakos did not explain, but turned to an underling. "Summon the elders of the tribe", he said. Then he turned to face Aldihoc. "Lord King, please allow Prince Ottoghar to offer you hospitality while we remedy this situation."

"You have won the right to take your time, Lord Abdarakos", Aldihoc replied, his shoulders slumped.

The erilar nodded to Ottoghar, who led Aldihoc and his retinue away towards his camp.

One by one the elders of the tribe arrived. "You will be at my side, Ragnar", Abdarakos said, "as will the shaman."

When all were seated on the furs inside the tent of the king, an old greybeard asked the obvious question, "Where is the king?"

"Summon Kursik the Hun", my grandsire said, and I left to do his bidding.

To my surprise I found Kursik outside the tent. A man whom I recognised to be a ringman of Rodolph stood beside the Hun. The warrior's hands were tied behind his back, he was gagged and had a rope around his neck, which I identified as Kursik's lasso.

Kursik dragged the bound man into the tent and pushed him to his knees in the centre of the gathering. He removed the lasso from around the warrior's neck, took his dagger in his fist, severed the ropes, and removed the gag.

In the event that the man had mischief on his mind, Kursik remained three paces away, his dagger drawn.

"Tell the truth and I will return your weapons and give you a good horse and provisions for ten days", the erilar growled. There was no need to state the alternative, as it was not difficult to divine.

The warrior nodded. "I accept, lord", he said.

"Where is the king?" Abdarakos asked.

"He has travelled east, lord", he said.

"Where to?"

For a span of heartbeats the man did not answer, then his shoulders slumped and he continued. "To the court of Prince Theoderic of the Ostrogoths", he revealed.

All around, elders gasped in shock.

"Why?" Abdarakos continued.

"Because he feared that his treachery would be revealed this morning, lord."

Abdarakos signalled for Kursik to remove the warrior from our presence. "Return his arms and see to it that he is given a good horse and provisions."

Objections rose from the assembled elders, but Abdarakos silenced them with a glare. "I have spoken", he growled, and none dared defy him. They knew that Abdarakos held the destiny of the tribe, as well as their lives, in the palm of his hand.

One of the braver elders said, "We are in your debt, war leader, but will you now grab the power and make yourself a king?"

"Do you object?" Abdarakos asked and his hand came to rest on the hilt of his blade.

Before the elder, who wore a concerned expression, could answer, Abdarakos continued.

"Once I have concluded a tributary agreement with Aldihoc, I will leave these lands, never to return." He gestured to Atakam. "The seer has seen the runes that the norns have painted on the bole of the world tree. My destiny lies elsewhere and I will be obedient to the gods."

"Then you will leave us to choose our own king?" he asked.

Atakam was the one who answered. "The gods have decreed that the Heruli must never have a king again."

244

"Then who will lead us?" the elders asked.

"We will elect a new war leader", the erilar said.

"He wants his grandson, Ragnar, as war leader", another elder shouted.

"Who better?" a greybeard replied. "Do you not know what he did yesterday? Are you deaf that you have not heard the rumours of his accomplishments? He has the blood of the khan!" But there were a few who shouted, "I remember him as a cripple", and, "Is he not the man who murdered a general of the East Romans?" A fierce argument erupted between the elders, which Abdarakos allowed to continue for a while.

"Silence!" the erilar eventually shouted.

"The one who must be the war leader is Ottoghar, son of King Edukon. He is of noble blood – a warrior prince of our kin, the Scirii. Ottoghar is an officer of Rome, where he is called Tribune Flavius Odovaker. The remnants of his people will flock to his banner, bolstering our armies. He will draft our warriors into the armies of Rome from where they will return with purses bulging with gold. He commands the loyalty of the mighty Rugii, and calls Prince Ferderuchus his friend. There are few tribes who would dare risk the ire of a man who leads the armies of the Rugii, Heruli and Rome."

"But more important than that – he has not forgotten who our true enemies are. Ottoghar has no love for the oathbreaking Ostrogoths or the treacherous Longobardi."

The erilar sneered at the assembled elders, who recoiled in fear. "And most important of all, he is not from one of your factions. He will show no favour and only act in the best interest of the tribe."

Needless to say, before the sun set that evening, the Heruli had elected a new war leader – Tribune Flavius Odovaker.

Chapter 30 – Wolves (August 473 AD)

Prince Ottoghar wore a bronze muscled cuirass over his undyed tunic. Draped around his broad, muscular shoulders was a red woollen cloak in the style preferred by Roman officers. He was clean-shaven and his hair cropped short in the way of the legions of old.

It had been more than a month since King Aldihoc had agreed to Abdarakos's terms. The Heruli were at peace with their neighbours - the Rugii to the south, the Longobardi to the north and the Gepids to the east.

Abdarakos raised his eyebrows at the decidedly Roman appearance of the war leader of the Heruli. "Tribune Flavius Odovaker", he said, and acknowledged the prince with a nod.

Prince Ottoghar suppressed a grin when the erilar used his Roman name. "The wolves are descending", he said, holding aloft a scroll bearing the seal of the emperor of the West. "The Visigoths have breached the western borders of the Empire. Emperor Glycerius has requested my presence to discourage King Euric of the Visigoths to advance into Italia from Gaul."

"Will you bolster your army with Heruli warriors?" the erilar asked.

"Now that there is peace, our warriors will wish to earn gold and loot", Odovaker confirmed with a nod. "I will give them the opportunity to join my banner. The same goes for the Rugii."

"And you have come to ask Abdarakos whether he wishes to join you", Atakam said.

Ottoghar issued a smile. "It is too late in the season to venture north", he said. "You will not be able to return to the far shores of Scandza until the Austmarr becomes navigable. Come, join me, we will winter in Italia where the climes are agreeable. We will feast on the riches of the Empire, redden our blades with the blood of Goths, and drink wine from the cellar of the emperor."

Ottoghar had a way with words. I may have been mistaken, but I believe I noticed Kursik wipe his mouth with his sleeve, no doubt salivating at the alluring prospect.

A week later we rode south. Ottoghar, or rather Tribune Odovaker, which was his preferred form of address within the borders of the Empire, led us from camp. Apart from his two thousand Scirii, one thousand Suebian cavalry and a thousand mounted Herulian lancers, he had managed to draw another thousand Rugii and two thousand Heruli foot to his banner.

Prince Ferderuchus rode abreast of Ottoghar. Abdarakos and Atakam followed close behind, with Kursik, Beremud, Boarex and me taking up the rear.

Three days earlier, Mourdagos, the larger-than-life war leader of the Boat Heruli, had led his men north, their boats filled with plunder gained from the Longobardi camp. Prince Ferderuchus, his reputation much enhanced, was on his way to the lands of the Rugii, but decided to travel with us for the first few days.

We rode in silence, and my thoughts drifted to Trokondas and his companion, the big excubitor Asbadus. My friend and mentor had willingly returned to the East to stand by the side of his brother, Illus. I knew that they would confront Zeno about his treachery and I prayed to the gods that it would not cost them their lives.

I had realised years before that we are all playthings in the hands of the gods, but what I did not know was that my fate was still entwined with that of Trokondas. We were both swept up in the torrent of life, but unbeknown to us, around a far bend in the river, the white water awaited. But it was not the foaming rapids that would be the problem, it was what would come after - a sheer precipice over which the water tumbled into oblivion.

"Tell me about King Euric of the Visigoths", I said when I found myself riding between Odovaker and Ferderuchus.

"He murdered his brother to gain the throne", Ferderuchus said.

For a moment I could not help but think of the acrimonious relationship between the Rugii prince and his own brother, Feva. Wisely I kept my mouth shut.

"Euric did not renew the *foedus* agreement with Rome when he came to power", Odovaker added. "After he united the warring factions within the Visigoth tribe, he started plundering Roman Gaul. Two years ago, Emperor Anthemius sent his son to Gaul with a mighty army at his back, but Euric defeated them, slaying the emperor's son and his tribal commanders."

"Surely the armies of Roman Gaul are powerful enough to hold the Visigoths at bay?" I asked.

"They are strong", Odovaker said, "but divided."

"In Avaricum there is Riothamus, the great lord of the Bretons, the men from Britain who have settled in the west of Gaul and are allied to the Alani. Riothamus commands a warband of three thousand heavy horsemen – a skilled and deadly force."

"Then there are the lands south of the Loire and north of Hispania controlled by the emperor of the West. The one who seems to wield the power is a senator by the name of Sidonius Apollinaris. He also happens to be the bishop of Averna."

"Syagrius, the Roman, controls the north of Gaul, the lands across the Loire. He tells all that he is but a provincial governor - alas, he is a self-styled king. He commands a numerous army of battle-hardened veterans. His neighbours to the north, the Franks, have asked Syagrius to lead their armies while their own king remains in exile."

"The Burgundians are firm allies of Rome. There is little they will enjoy more than unleashing the horde against the Visigoths. But they are fearful to stand alone."

"If all of these warlords were to unite under the banner of Rome, even the innumerable horde of Euric will tremble in fear. But alas, Rome only pursues its own agenda. Why did Anthemius send his son to face Euric on his own? Because he wished for his son to win glory – glory that would have strengthened his rule. No, my friends. The Western Empire is crumbling, and still the emperors think only of themselves."

"Then why are we riding south?" I asked. "If all is lost."

"Gaul is all but lost", Odovaker said. "But not Italia. If nothing is done, the Visigoths will overrun not only Gaul, but also the whole of Italia. If the Goths gain power, they will turn on the old allies of Attila. We will be banished to the lands north of the Danube while Euric will lay claim to the riches of the Empire."

"The wolves best be careful", Atakam said. "The beast is wounded, but it is still a bear."

Chapter 31 – Italia

"Attila's handiwork", Abdarakos said, gesturing to the blackened ruins of what once was one of the finest cities in all of the Roman world.

The old warlord issued a snicker. "We almost abandoned the siege", he said. "Almost. But the great khan inspired us. Our purses overflowed with gold after we breached the walls of Aquileia."

For a while he stared at the ruins, trying to reconstruct the razed city in his mind. He pointed to a heap of rubble where three peasants were loading cut stone and marble cladding onto the back of a cart. "There!" he exclaimed. "That's where we breached the wall."

The peasants, thinking that the scarred warlord was pointing at them, fell to their knees. "We're not stealing the stone, m'lord", one explained. "It's for the bishop himself, m'lord. His holiness is rebuilding the church, m'lord."

We ignored the ramblings of the man and spurred our horses back towards the Via Postuma, heading west to catch up with Odovaker and his men. It had taken us close to four weeks to reach Aquileia, just barely able to cross the treacherous Alps along the Pear Tree Pass, south of Emona, before the snow arrived in earnest.

On our return to the main host, Odovaker signalled for us to join him in the vanguard.

"I have received a missive from Arelate in Gaul", the tribune said. "A Visigoth force is heading east on the Via Domitia towards the Alpine passes that lead to Italia. Arelate has closed its gates to the enemy because the garrison is not powerful enough to halt them. Euric's army is led by a general named Vincentius."

Odovaker continued with pursed lips. "Vincentius used to be the Roman high general of Hispania, but he saw the writing on the wall and now serves Euric."

"Is he a man of reputation?" Abdarakos asked.

Odovaker nodded. "Unfortunately, he is."

"Most seasons, the Via Domitia is the last of the Alpine passes to be blocked by snow", he added. "It will remain traversable for at least another six weeks."

"My Greek tutor had once told me that a mighty general of old, on his way from Carthage, crossed the Alps in the middle of winter", I said.

Odovaker shook his head. "I've been up those passes in late autumn", he replied. "Don't believe everything that the Greeks tell you."

Abdarakos ignored the jibe. "How long will it take the Goths to reach Italia?" he asked.

"Three weeks at the least", Odovaker said. "When they spill from the passes, we must be there to meet them."

* * *

On the day, three weeks later, we sighted the massive tower-studded stone walls of Augusta Taurinorum. While Odovaker went to speak with the city prefect, we made camp on a flat piece of ground north of the fortress, on the banks of the Po River.

The city fathers' joy at our arrival was evident judging by the multitude of wagons, heaped with food and wine, that accompanied Odovaker on his return to camp. Later that evening he joined us around the fire.

"Gaul is like a putrefied foot", Odovaker said, and spat out the pip of another succulent olive. "I have seen men die terrible deaths because of their unwillingness to have a medicus remove a limb -

one already purple from *gangraina*. Till the bitter end they believe that the gods will heal them." He took a swallow of wine, shrugged, and continued. "Of course, they always die."

"It is the same with Rome. Gaul used to be the pride of the Empire, but now it has been tainted by the Visigoth curse. Cut it off, I say, before the whole of Italia is polluted by the Gothic affliction."

Abdarakos was not afraid to contradict Odovaker. "Roman warriors have shed rivers of blood to conquer Gaul", he said. "One should not be in too much of a hurry to give up land that was conquered by the sword."

Odovaker sighed. "You are not wrong, Lord Abdarakos", he said, "but I do not believe that the factions can be united against the Goths."

"Why don't you try?" Abdarakos said, and took a swig of wine, his gaze remaining fixed on Odovaker.

Before Odovaker could answer, a scout arrived to report.

"The Goths will be here in two, maybe three days, tribune", he said.

"Numbers?" the tribune asked.

When the warrior did not meet Odovaker's eyes, I knew that the tidings would not be good.

"They outnumber us, lord", he said.

"They are well armoured?" the tribune asked.

The scout nodded. "With chain, scale and helmets, lord. When they march, it is like a river of iron."

Odovaker dismissed the scout with a wave of his hand and turned to face Abdarakos, who stood beside me. "The Goths have been fighting in Gaul and Hispania for many years", he said. "The warriors whom we will face are veterans all - survivors of countless battles. Many of the Roman soldiers have joined their ranks."

"We need shock cavalry to counter their heavily armoured footmen", the erilar growled.

Odovaker remained silent for a moment, no doubt deep in thought. "Seventy years ago, when King Alaric led his horde of Visigoths across the Alps, the famous Roman general of barbarian birth, Stilicho, defeated the Goths not twenty miles south of here", he said. "As a reward for their service, the warriors who gave him victory were allowed to settle with their families near the site of the battle, close to Pollentium. They prosper, and can field more than a thousand warriors."

257

"Who are they?" I asked.

"Alani", Odovaker replied. "Sarmatian heavy cavalry who wield the armour-piercing, two-handed lance. Two dukes command them – Alla and Sindila."

A frown settled on Abdarakos's scarred brow. "Then why have you not asked them for assistance?" he growled.

"Because Alla and Sindila have sworn to kill me", Odovaker replied.

Sensing the start of a tale, Abdarakos filled Odovaker's cup to the brim.

"My patron, mentor and friend was the man you know as Ricimer", he said. "Ricimer was the product of a marriage between the royal houses of the Suebi and the Visigoths. It was ordained that he would unite the people and become a great ruler. His grandfather, King Wallia of the Visigoths, was a fierce warrior and a prudent and wise ruler. When Wallia was murdered by a usurper, the boy Ricimer and his mother were forced to flee to Rome to escape the same fate."

"Although barbarian blood coursed through Ricimer's veins, he was a Roman in his heart. Having inherited his grandfather's talents, he rose through the ranks of the army. Soon he was the

258

understudy of General Flavius Aetius, the only man who had ever been able to stand his ground against the great khan."

"But another young man, a true Roman, also learned warcraft from the famous General Aetius. This man's name was Majorian. He was a gifted strategist and a fierce warrior. But even Majorian could not compete against the blood of kings, and before long Ricimer was Aetius's favourite. Rather than become jealous of each other, Ricimer and Majorian became friends, as close as brothers."

"When General Aetius was treacherously murdered by Emperor Valentinian, the Empire was all but doomed. But Ricimer and Majorian joined forces to save Rome. Ricimer knew that, due to his barbarian blood, he would never be accepted as emperor, so he made a pact with Majorian. Majorian would rule, while Ricimer would be his sword."

"Once they had seized power, they defeated one enemy after another. They reconquered the lost territories of Hispania and Southern Gaul, and subjugated the Visigoths, Suebi and Burgundians."

"Things took a turn for the worse when Majorian succumbed to delusions of grandeur. He viewed himself as a new Julius Caesar, believing that he could restore the Empire to its former glory. But he ignored the fact that the treasury had barely enough funds to pay the barbarian foederati who fought the Empire's wars. He used the last of the gold to build a fleet of three hundred ships, planning on sailing to Carthage to destroy King Geiseric and his Vandals. Ricimer advised against it, but Majorian refused to listen to his counsel."

"When Majorian was about to set sail, Geiseric attacked the Roman fleet in the port. After Majorian neglected to pay the captains, Geiseric bribed them to defect to his banner. The ships Geiseric did not capture, he destroyed."

"Having concluded a disgraceful truce, Majorian stopped over in Gaul on his way back to Rome and held games and feasts in his own honour, ignoring the crushing defeat. He disbanded the enormous barbarian army he had recruited and sent the warriors home without pay and without the spoils of war."

Abdarakos shook his head. "If there is no victory, no gold and no spoils, the men of the tribes blame the leader of the army. It is their way."

Odovaker nodded his agreement.

"The Alani, who was part of Majorian's army, returned to Italia. The warriors had spent the summer away from home, unable to tend to their flocks. They returned home with empty purses, facing starving wives and children. Reverting to what they knew best, they raided Roman farms in order to sustain themselves."

He drank deeply from his cup and shrugged. "Who can blame them?"

"Majorian promised the Alani gold as long as they stopped raiding. He rode north to meet them, but secretly commanded Ricimer to slay them all."

"Majorian's actions incensed Ricimer, who intercepted the emperor at Dertona, and killed him."

"But why do the Alani wish to kill you?" I asked.

Odovaker raised a hand. "Let me finish", he said and took another swig to wet his throat.

"When they heard that the emperor had been slain, the Alani continued their depredations. They believed that Ricimer slew Majorian and stole the gold meant for the Alani. Of course, there had been no gold in the first place."

"The Alani refused to listen to reason, and Ricimer crushed their revolt. A young warrior slew their leader, Beogar, who was the father of Alla and Sindila."

"And who is the warrior you speak about?" Abdarakos asked.

"That young warrior was me", Odovaker said.

Chapter 32 – Alani

Abdarakos dismounted and removed his gilded helmet with both hands. I swung down from the saddle and accepted the proffered reins of his horse. He nodded, turned his back to me, and started down the road.

Two hundred paces away, three Alani thundered towards us. They were mounted on large warhorses, which, like their riders, were encased in leather and iron.

At a distance of seventy paces, the Alani lowered their long, heavy lances.

The erilar ignored their thundering advance and continued to walk in their direction. For a heartbeat I believed that the warriors would simply run him through, but they reined in, the tip of the lead rider's lance two feet from Abdarakos's mailed chest.

My grandsire did not stop, but continued walking until the blade of the spear pressed against the iron scales, willing the warrior to stand down.

The lead rider handed his lance to an underling and removed his helmet. "You are far from home, Heruli", he said in the language of the Steppes.

"And so are you, Alani", the erilar growled. "I am Abdarakos, general of the great khan."

Then, to my surprise, the horseman swung from the saddle. He strode towards my grandsire and went down onto one knee.

"I failed to recognise you, lord", the Alani said. "Up until his last days, my father told tales of your exploits together."

"I hear that Beogar has fallen, Sindila", the erilar replied.

A dark cloud seemed to settle on Sindila's face. "My father died a warrior's death", he said, "and will be content in the afterlife. But his murder remains unavenged."

Sindila gestured for Abdarakos to follow him. "But let us not speak of the dead, lord", he said. "Come, join us around the fire and share a cup of wine."

While we followed the Alani to their camp, Abdarakos told me the tale.

"When Attila crossed the Alps, I led the forces that besieged Aurelianum in Roman Gaul", he explained. "The old Alani king, Goar, was a wise ruler. He sent emissaries to me, agreeing to open the gates of the city to Attila on condition that we spared his people. He sent his favourite son, Beogar, along as a hostage. But a rival noble in the city, a warrior called Sangiban, supported by the Visigoths, usurped the throne before we reached Aurelianum. The new Alani king closed the gates to us."

"By rights I could have killed Beogar, but I knew that he was not to blame. He joined my retinue and fought at my side against the Goths and the usurper, Sangiban, who had murdered his father. After Attila's death, Beogar joined his people in Italia and became their leader."

That evening, we sat cross-legged around the fire in the company of Alla and Sindila, the sons of Beogar. At their behest, Abdarakos told the tale of the greatest battle of our time - the battle of the Catalaunian Plains.

He stared into the fire for long, with sadness in his eyes. Finally, he spoke, rage dripping from his lips. "The Visigoths placed their new allies, the Alani under Sangiban, in the centre where they faced the great khan and his most ferocious fighters. That is where your father and I fought – at the side of Attila. No matter how hard we tried, we were unable to breach the line of the Alani."

I could not help but notice pride in the eyes of Alla and Sindila, who hung onto the erilar's words.

"Thousands of the bravest men died that day", Abdarakos continued. "Horse warrior pitted against horse warrior – all men who had once called the Sea of Grass their home."

"The Ostrogoths, our allies then, fought on the khan's left wing, facing the Visigoths. The Ostrogoths broke, allowing the Visigoths to fall upon our flank. They came for Attila himself, wishing to slay the great khan, but they had not taken into account the quality of the men who surrounded the king. At twilight we cut a bloody path through the Visigoth ranks and retreated to our camp."

For a span of heartbeats Abdarakos breathed deeply, and it was clear that he tried to calm himself. Then he drained his cup and leaned in closer, lowering his voice. "When the khan was safe, I went in search of Valamir, the king of the Ostrogoths, because I suspected treachery. Why did their line break so easily?"

"And who did I find entering the tent of Valamir of the Ostrogoths? None other than Thorismund, prince of the Visigoths."

"I went to Attila, and that night, in secret, we met with Aetius, the great general of Rome."

"As a boy, Aetius had been raised at the court of the king of the Huns. Although he was a purebred Roman, he respected the ways of the tribes", Abdarakos said. "He told us that his ally, Thorismund of the Visigoths, had pleaded with him to fall upon the camp of Attila the following day."

"In the end, it was not difficult to figure out. The Ostrogoths and Visigoths had secretly planned to turn on their allies once Attila was dead. First they would fall on the Romans, then they would unite the leaderless tribes under the banner of the Goths."

"Aetius and Attila clasped arms that night, promising to end the hostilities."

"The following morning the king of the Visigoths was found dead. They say that he had died in the fierce battle of the previous day, but I knew better. Like the great khan, Aetius had little patience for treachery, and I still believe that the Goth king died by the Roman general's blade."

We all sat in silence, shocked at the revelation of the erilar.

Abdarakos took the thick golden torque from his neck. "Swear that you will never repeat the words that I have spoken."

Alla, Sindila and I did as we were told. Only a fool would refuse a man with the reputation of Abdarakos.

The two Alani were in awe of the erilar. He went on to tell them about the treachery of Majorian – how Ricimer and Odovaker were not to be blamed for the death of their father, Beogar. In their hearts he kindled a new fire to replace the oath of vengeance. The following morning when we departed, the flame of hatred for the Goths burned brightly.

Although I believe that all my grandsire had told them was true, I realised why Abdarakos, great lord of the Heruli, was such a formidable warlord. His legendary adroitness with the blade was equalled, if not surpassed, by his skill with the tongue.

Chapter 33 – Donar

The eastern side of the Susa Valley, Northern Italy, where the Col de Montgenevre Pass spills into the Valley of the Po.

The flat land just north of the Avigliani Lakes, bordered by Monte Capretto to the south, the Dora Riparia River to the east and the foothills of the Cottian Alps to the west.

Abdarakos, Odovaker, Atakam and I sat in the saddle. From our vantage point, near the base of a hill, overlooking the flat ground to the north, the entire battlefield was visible. It was early afternoon, the weather unusually warm for the time of year.

A few paces away, Kursik, Boarex and Beremud, like us, were observing the enemy's deployment.

"Do the Alani still wish to slit my throat?" Odovaker asked offhandedly while we watched the Visigoth army of the Roman general array for battle.

"It is possible", Abdarakos replied, his eyes fixed on the enemy lines.

The battlefield that lay before us was less than a mile wide. To the west, the forested foothills of the Alps anchored our left flank.

To the east, the Dora Riparia River protected the approach from the right.

My grandsire pointed to the three blocks of heavy infantry that made up the centre, left and right of the Goth army. "Eight thousand in total", he said. "They are all encased in iron. See how orderly they deploy. General Vincentius has given them discipline, transformed them into Romans."

In addition to the infantry, a thousand medium horsemen protected each flank of the foe.

Odovaker had placed his thousand Rugii footmen in the centre. The two thousand Heruli infantry formed the right flank while the Scirii heavy foot were stationed on the left. To counter the cavalry of the enemy, the Heruli mounted lancers protected our left flank and the Suebian cavalry our right.

"Vincentius will notice how thin our ranks are in the centre", Abdarakos said.

"And like any competent Roman general he will be schooled in the art of war", Odovaker added. "He will believe that we wish for him to push our weak centre back so we are able to fall on his flanks. It is a strategy favoured by the Goths."

The tribune had hardly uttered the words when a note from a buccina echoed across the plain, triggering movement within the ranks of the enemy.

"They suspect a trap", Abdarakos said. "Look, they are strengthening their flanks at the cost of their centre."

"Good", Odovaker said.

Vincentius was a cautious general. He realised that his forces outnumbered ours, and that, bar an error in judgement on his side, his veterans would no doubt carry the day.

As soon as Vincentius was satisfied, the buccina sounded the advance. The standards of the Goths bobbed up and down as the wall of spear-wielding warriors approached our ranks like a flood of iron.

I was so enthralled by the happenings in front of us and the conversation between Odovaker and Abdarakos to my left, I had forgotten all about the old shaman on my right. When I stole a glance at Atakam, I noticed that he had turned his horse around, facing away from the battle, staring up at the sky behind us. I reached out and touched my grandsire's arm to draw his attention. He turned to face me, a frown creasing his brow on account of the distraction. Then he, too, noticed Atakam staring at the heavens.

Soon all eyes were on the shaman, who spoke without averting his gaze.

"It is the gods who will decide the outcome of the battle", he said. "Is it not so?"

He received no reply to the contrary and continued. "Then why are you so concerned by the actions of mere mortals?" he asked. "Does it not make sense to rather seek the counsel of the gods?"

We turned our horses around, ignoring the flood of spears and iron bearing down on us.

"Look!" the shaman exclaimed, pointing at the slate-grey clouds bunching above our heads, which threatened to blot out the sun. "Do you not see?" he all but shouted. "Donar, great lord of war and thunder, favours us", he proclaimed, and raised both his arms in the air. Just then, a bolt of lightning split the sky and less than a heartbeat later a mighty roar of thunder shook the earth.

"There", the shaman said. "Do you need more?"

Odovaker, momentarily captivated by the shaman, was brought back to the present by the clap of thunder. We all turned around, the enemy having closed the gap between the armies to a hundred paces. He nodded to his signifier, a note echoed across the battlefield, and our warriors advanced to meet the foe.

Before the two front ranks came together, the thousand Heruli mounted lancers on our right flank did the unexpected. They turned their horses around and retreated to the rear of the infantry.

The feigned retreat was a well-known tactic of the eastern nomads. The withdrawal of our cavalry on the left made our flank vulnerable to attack. But the Roman general was too shrewd a commander to jeopardize his nearly unassailable advantage for the benefit of an easy victory.

The Gothic cavalry displayed their iron discipline and remained to guard their own right flank, unconcerned about the lancers' repositioning. Vincentius would use the superior numbers of his infantry to grind us down, little by little. But what the Roman general did not know, was that it was exactly what we had hoped for.

The fleet-of-foot Rugii narrowed their frontage, allowing a column of Heruli mounted lancers, fifty horses wide and twenty deep, to face the enemy charge. The horsemen did not rush the shield wall of the approaching Goths, but kept pace with our infantry. It had been a favourite tactic of Attila's – to face infantry with mounted, shield-bearing lancers.

The line of mounted lancers pushed up against the enemy infantry line, pressing against their shields with the armoured breasts of their horses. From horseback they were afforded a loftier view, while their long armour-piercing weapons provided a deadly reach.

Many horses and riders fell in the press, but the Heruli relentlessly dug their spurs into the sides of their horses – the animals instinctively surging forward, too tightly pressed to flee to the rear. But no human warriors can absorb the sustained pressure from immensely powerful horses while being stabbed from above. Inevitably the lancers broke the Gothic line and spilled into the gap.

To his credit, Vincentius kept his wits about him. When he noticed the breach, his infantry reserve rushed towards the point of weakness, reinforcing the ranks.

Vincentius must have realised that the bold move of Odovaker had shifted the momentum against the Goths. To regain the upper hand he responded in kind, ordering his cavalry to fall upon our unprotected flank.

Odovaker had anticipated this, and stationed his best warriors on the left. But even champions cannot halt a flanking attack from medium cavalry, and slowly but surely the foe bested our warriors. Or so it appeared.

Meanwhile, the storm had arrived in all its glory. Flashes of lightning illuminated the darkened sky and thunder shook the earth. The rumble of the god of thunder masked the sound of the approach of the two thousand heavy Alani horsemen emerging from their hiding place behind Monte Capretto.

By the time that the Goth cavalry assailing our flank noticed the wall of armoured horseflesh thundering down on them, their fate was already sealed. The Goth riders cast their javelins in a desperate attempt to avoid the inevitable, but the missiles had little effect. Sindila's thousand horsemen crushed the enemy cavalry with a single charge while Alla's men drove deep into the ranks of the Goth footmen, annihilating nearly half of their right flank. When their charge was halted by the heaped corpses of the foe, they reached for their flanged maces and continued the slaughter.

I stole a glance to my right and was not surprised to see that Atakam was the only man not facing the field of blood. The eyes of the shaman were still focused on the heavens above.

* * *

Odovaker pressed his golden seal ring onto the blob of red bitumen. "Read it", he commanded his secretary, who warily eyed the hulking Alani commanders whose scale armour were spattered with Goth blood.

The Greek secretary cleared his throat and read the words out loud.

"My lord Glycerius Augustus,

I wish to confirm that the forces of the Visigoth invaders, led by the traitor Vincentius, have suffered a grievous defeat near Augusta Taurinorum at the hands of the Alani dukes, Alla and Sindila.

The scattered remnants of King Euric's army have fled across the passes to Gaul, but Vincentius has been slain.

Your humble servant.

Tribune Flavius Odovaker"

Abdarakos nodded his approval. "Tribune Odovaker has not only relinquished his share of the loot", he said, "but also his share of the glory."

"You have shown yourself to be a man of honour, Tribune Odovaker", Sindila said. "The erilar has opened our eyes to who the real enemy is."

When Alla and Sindila had departed with their spoils, Odovaker dismissed his underlings.

"The passes will still be open for a few weeks", he said, gesturing at the clear blue skies. "I will heed your advice, Lord Abdarakos. My men will remain at Augusta Taurinorum for the winter, while I travel to Gaul to see whether the enemies of the Visigoths can be united. Join me, and I will arrange for a ship to take you north, to the lands of the Boat Heruli, when the sea becomes navigable in spring."

Chapter 34 – Gaul (September 473 AD)

A few miles east of Averna (Augusto Nemetum), central Gaul.

(Modern day Clermont-Ferrand, France.)

A man wearing a thick-woven, dark brown cloak trundled down the cobbled road. An ample hood concealed his face, even though the large silver cross swinging from a leather thong around his neck clearly identified him as a servant of the Roman God.

"Lord", I said in my best Latin when he drew level with us.

The hooded figure's head jerked towards the sound, but in the grey twilight he failed to notice our hiding place in the shadows at the side of the forested path.

"Lord bishop", I said again, and we stepped out into the open.

He stared at my face for a short time, then drank in the scarred visage of Kursik.

"Take me to your master, Herulian", he said, ignoring my Hun friend.

He spoke in a tone one would use when addressing a thrall, but I took little offence as I had been forewarned by Odovaker.

I smiled when I recalled the tribune's words. "Not only is he a bishop", Odovaker had said, "but also an important man descended from an ancient noble family. In their hearts the Romans still believe that they are better than us. Take no heed of it."

He noticed my amusement and sneered, "Your master will hear of your insolence. I will demand that you be punished, heathen."

"Kill him", I told Kursik, and translated my words for the benefit of our guest.

The Hun made a show of sliding a curved dagger from the scabbard tied to his belt, the blade glinting in the fading light. He took a step towards the bishop, who staggered backwards.

I stalled Kursik by placing my hand on his shoulder. "One more word, bishop", I growled, "and I will tell Tribune Odovaker that you never arrived."

Needless to say, the remainder of our journey was completed in silence.

Odovaker was waiting for us outside the tent he had set up for the clandestine meeting. Before he turned his attention to the tribune,

Bishop Sidonius Apollinaris fixed me with a leering glance, which carried a promise of revenge.

"I have prayed to our Lord to protect you, tribune", he said and extended his right hand towards the Scirii prince, who bent down and kissed the large golden episcopal ring set with a red amethyst.

"As have I, your grace", Odovaker replied, leaving me confused to whether he had beseeched the Christian God for the safekeeping of himself or the bishop.

Bishop Apollinaris hesitated for a moment, no doubt sharing my concern, then nodded, giving the benefit of the doubt to Odovaker. "Thank you, my child", he said.

The tribune bade the bishop to enter, who again made sure he leered at me, removing all vestiges of doubt from my mind that he intended to insist on some form of reprisal.

Odovaker noticed the unspoken exchange. "By the sake of the gods, Ragnar", he said once the Roman had entered. "What did you do to him?"

"I told Kursik to kill him", I said, and followed the bishop inside the tent before the Scirii prince could reply.

Inside the dimly lit tent, Abdarakos was seated beside a central hearth. "This is the man who commands the loyalty of the Herulians", Odovaker said, indicating my grandsire.

The bishop, aware of the barbarian way, inclined his head to the erilar.

"And this is the son of Ildiko", Odovaker said, gesturing in my direction.

It took a moment for the bishop to realise the significance of the words. His eyes widened at the revelation, but he was no fool and inclined his head, giving no hint to our earlier disagreement.

We had hardly taken our places on the furs when another hooded person entered the tent. Although the hulking figure wore a cloak, it was clear that he was a warrior.

"Lord Riothamus of the Bretons", the bishop exclaimed when the man threw back the hood of his cloak to reveal a scarred, yet handsome face, framed by shoulder-length blonde hair and a neatly trimmed beard.

"Lord Apollinaris", Riothamus said in perfect Latin, acknowledging the bishop.

The bishop introduced us to the Breton as if he had known us for years, not mere heartbeats.

Flavius Odovaker was not a man inclined to small talk and took the bull by the horns. "Alone, we are not strong enough to resist the Gothic menace", Odovaker said. "But if Roman and Breton unite, we will crush the army of King Euric."

The great lord of the Bretons was cut from the same cloth. "Three years ago", Riothamus growled, "the Romans sent a letter to Euric, asking him to squash the Bretons under his heel. Now, you beg for my sword?"

Bishop Apollinaris raised both his open palms, fingers spread wide, in a gesture indicating his innocence. "The praetorian prefect of Gaul acted without the emperor's consent. He was tried and found guilty", he said. "Arvandus paid with his life."

"Conveniently", Riothamus replied and raised a hand to stall a response. "But even if the Bretons joined with Rome, we will still not be strong enough to defeat the Goths. You will need to convince Syagrius, the Roman king of the lands north of the Loire, to join us. Only if you are able to do that, will I call my people to war."

Before anyone could offer a reply, the great lord of the Bretons stood from the furs. "I have spoken", he said. "And my mind

will not be changed by talk. Send word if you achieve what I
have asked. Else, leave me be."

He paid his respects to all in the room and departed without
another word.

"Can Syagrius be convinced?" the bishop asked.

"No", Odovaker replied. "Ricimer ordered the killing of
Syagrius's father, Aegidius. He despises everyone who called my
mentor a friend. Syagrius would rather join the Goths than us."

Abdarakos, who had listened to all that was said, spoke for the
first time. "Syagrius, I am told, is the war leader of the Franks.
The strength of his rule is derived from the sword arms of the
warriors of that mighty nation."

Apollinaris nodded. "The Franks have a king", he said. "But
eight years ago, he was exiled to the lands of the Thuringians. I
heard that it was a plot of Syagrius and his father Aegidius."

Abdarakos smiled then. "I have met Childeric of the Franks", he
said. "When he was but a boy, a hostage at the court of Attila."

"The khan was a shrewd man", the erilar continued. "He
appointed a Hun, Wiomad, as the boy's tutor. When Childeric
left Attila's court, Wiomad travelled with the boy to the lands of

Frankia. It is said that Wiomad became like a father to Childeric."

"We must seek out this man, Wiomad", Abdarakos said. "Maybe a deal can be made which will benefit all."

* * *

"Tell Wiomad who your father is", the erilar said. "Show him the horn bow of the great khan and he will know that you speak the truth."

I nodded, feeling the weight of the responsibility settle on my shoulders.

"Kursik will travel with you", Abdarakos said. "It is not safe to traverse the Realm of Syagrius. Go east, through the lands of the Burgundians", he commanded. "Odovaker will give you a scroll – he is acquainted with King Gundobad."

"From there, journey north through the lands of the Alemanni. Their king, Gibuld, is a friend of the Heruli."

"What about Boarex and Beremud?" I asked.

"Atakam and I have need of them", he said with a sly smile, and told me what he had in mind.

* * *

Tornacum, Frankia, formerly part of Roman Gallia Belgica (Modern day Tournai, France)

Perplexed, the old man accepted the Hun bow and reverently ran his fingers along the intricate silver inlays of swirling animal motifs. "Only one like this was ever made", he whispered. For a moment I was convinced that he was about to start crying.

But when he succeeded in tearing his gaze from the weapon, an angry frown furrowed his brow. "Where did you get this, Herulian?" he growled.

"It belonged to my father", I said.

Wiomad did not respond for a span of heartbeats as he digested my answer. "Who is your mother?" he asked.

"Her name was Ildiko", I replied. "Daughter of Abdarakos, the war leader of the Heruli."

"And the wife of the great khan", he said, completing my sentence.

As if in a daze, he muttered, his words nearly inaudible, "The father of a great nation." Then he managed to extract himself from his reverie. "Why are you here, son of Attila?"

"I have a proposal for you, Lord Wiomad", I said.

He held up a hand to stall my response. "What is your name?" he asked.

"My name is Ragnar, lord", I replied.

"Come, Ragnar, son of Attila. First, we will share a cup while you tell me your tale", he said, and led me into his private quarters.

Two cups of mead later I had told all.

"If Childeric returns from exile, Syagrius will attack us before the young king is able to rally his lords", Wiomad said. "I will not tell him that it is safe to return only to have him slaughtered by the Roman king."

"But what if a large force of Saxons were to move up the River Loire?" I asked. "Would Syagrius not be forced to send his army south?"

Wiomad's eyes narrowed. "What influence have you over the northern raiders?" he asked.

"None", I replied. "But I know someone who does – Mourdagos, war leader of the Boat Heruli."

* * *

The old man reached for the gold chain that hung around his neck, and I noticed that a pendant was attached to it – a gold coin, crudely cut in half by a blow from an axe.

He held it out to me and I leaned down from atop the magnificent horse to allow him to place it around my neck. "Childeric has the other half", he said. "Look after it. Without it, he will not believe that I have sent you."

He stood back to allow us to depart, but then he spoke to Kursik. "Ragnar has the blood of the khan", he said. "I hope that he rides like a Hun?"

"Ragnar rides better than a Hun, lord", Kursik said, and spurred his horse not to fall behind.

Chapter 35 – Andecavus (March 474 AD)

The southern bank of the Loire River, across from the city of Andecavus on the northern bank. The southern boundary of the independent Roman kingdom of Syagrius, Western Gaul.

(Modern day Angers, France.)

Odovaker pointed at the forty-eight longships that slowly glided across the water of the Loire, heading towards the river wall of Andecavus.

"The Saxons will keep your army besieged for months", Odovaker said. "They will kill everyone outside the walls. If you give battle, you might lose half your men."

Beside Odovaker stood a man dressed in the style of the Romans - the warlord of King Syagrius, better known as Count Paul.

"And you will convince them to do otherwise?" Count Paul asked.

"I have come to speak with Childeric, the new war leader of the Franks", Odovaker replied. "He has promised to send his warriors south to join us in a campaign against the Goths."

"These Saxons, do you know them?" he asked again.

Odovaker gestured with his chin in my direction. "One of my foederati chieftains is kin of the Saxons", he said. "He might be able to persuade them to leave if they are given Roman gold."

"Is he a Saxon?" Count Paul asked, speaking about me as if I were not there.

"He is a Herul", Odovaker replied absentmindedly, studying the approaching fleet.

Count Paul's gaze was still fixed on me. "They all look the same to me", he sneered. "Be it Saxon, Herul or Dane – large, blonde, with ugly heathen faces despoiled with revolting green tattoos."

He turned to face the faraway ships, still inexorably rowing towards the city, and sighed, "What are your terms?"

"I need two thousand mounted lancers and the same number of heavy foot", Odovaker said. "That, and permission for the Franks to cross your lands."

Count Paul nodded. "Make sure the Saxons leave", he said, "and I will honour your request."

* * *

The southern bank of the Loire River, across from the city of Aurelianum on the northern bank. The southern boundary of the independent Roman kingdom of Syagrius, Western Gaul.

(Modern day Orléans, France)

Riothamus dismounted and flicked his reins to an underling. The great lord of the Bretons pulled the tight-fitting gilded iron helmet from his head and flexed his bull-like neck to rid himself of the stiffness of the long ride.

His armour was a mixture of Roman chain and the scale favoured by the Alani. The fierce-looking horsemen accompanying the Breton lord were no doubt of mixed blood.

He acknowledged us by inclining his head, then pointed at the city across the river. "The horde of the Franks are but a day's march north of here", he said. "The army of the Goths is marching to Avaricum, seventy miles to the southeast. They will arrive there in six days' time."

"Where do you suggest we give battle?" Odovaker asked.

"My scouts report that Euric's army is moving north, towards Argentomagus, where they will cross the River Creuse. From there they will head east along the main Roman road to

Avaricum. Southeast of Avaricum there is a plain where our horsemen will be most effective", Riothamus replied. "At the place the Romans call Dolensus, we will crush the Gothic horde."

Odovaker waved one of his men closer. "Take a message to Bishop Apollinaris. The Romans are to meet us at Avaricum. We will be there before the Goths arrive."

Count Paul, who commanded the forces of Syagrius, nodded. "We, too, will march tomorrow at first light."

When all had departed to go about their arrangements, I remained in the presence of Odovaker and Abdarakos. "How many men will we have?" I asked.

"Our own force numbers two thousand Scirii infantry, and two thousand Suebi and Herulian horsemen", the tribune replied. "The bishop's lords can field two thousand men – half cavalry and half infantry. Childeric of the Franks and Count Paul each command four thousand men, equally split between cavalry and infantry, while Riothamus has three thousand heavy riders."

"Seventeen thousand men", I said. "Of which ten thousand are horsemen."

"I have never doubted that Euric's army would outnumber us", Abdarakos said. "Only if we stand together will we prevail. When the tribes rose up against the sons of the khan, we were outnumbered - outnumbered against Huns! But we prevailed because on that fateful day at Nedao, we did not fight alongside men of other tribes, we fought shoulder to shoulder with our kin. There, on the field of blood, among the corpses, we became family – blood brothers till the end."

"Will it be the same when we meet the Visigoths?" I asked.

"We will see", Abdarakos said and exchanged a glance with Odovaker.

* * *

Outside the walls of Avaricum, Roman Gaul.

(Modern day Bourges, France)

Odovaker kneeled beside the blazing fire around which all the commanders of the allied forces were gathered. "Our scouts have confirmed the numbers of Euric's force", he said. "Twenty-five thousand, of which five thousand are mounted."

Using the tip of a broken spear, he drew a circle in the sand. "This is Avaricum", he said, and pointed at the massive, tower-

291

studded walls of the great Roman fortress. Starting at the circle, he drew a line in the sand, extending south. "From here we will move towards Dolensus where we will give battle to the Goths."

At the extremity of the line, he drew a large square. "The Goths will pursue us south. We will flee before them, but at Dolensus we will turn to face them."

Opposite the large square Odovaker drew a rectangle. "I will take the centre with my two thousand heavy infantry and two thousand horsemen."

"Cavalry against packed infantry?" Riothamus asked.

"Our ranks will have to be shallow, but we will hold them – we have faced heavy infantry with cavalry before. The bishop's men will support us to ensure that our line remains unbroken."

"I will command the right flank", Childeric said, and Odovaker nodded his approval.

"And I the left", Count Paul said, drawing the same response from the tribune.

Odovaker extended his arm and handed the broken spear to Riothamus, who drew a large circle south of Dolensus. "Here, an ancient forest of oak and beech blankets the hills", he said. "I will conceal my heavy cavalry amongst the trees and when the battle is raging and the Goths press you towards the edge of the forest, my horsemen will circle around their flank and smash into their ranks from behind."

* * *

Kursik and I fought shoulder to shoulder with the Herulian mounted lancers stationed on the far left side of the centre, which was under the command of Odovaker. To our left was the army of Count Paul.

I dragged my spurs along the flanks of my horse and felt the animal surge forward, its chest pressing against the shield wall of the Goths. A spear snaked from between two overlapped shields, striking my mount's head a glancing blow. But the iron-studded leather chamfron turned the point and caused my horse to surge forward. I grabbed the haft of the foe's spear a handsbreadth behind the point and jerked it towards me, while, at the same time, raising myself from the saddle using my leather stirrups. The Goth lost his balance and lowered his shield a few inches. My lance struck like lightning over the iron rim of his shield, piercing his neck below the guard of his helmet.

Another warrior stepped into the gap, and his sword blade flashed low, aimed at the unprotected legs of my horse. But Kursik's lasso whipped across from my left and tightened around the Goth's neck before the screaming warrior was dragged to his doom.

We held out against the overwhelming numbers for long. In spite of our efforts, slowly but surely we were being pressed back towards the treeline at our rear.

Odovaker's signifier issued a note on the buccina, and I knew that the time had come to unleash Riothamus and his heavy cavalry. Again, we were forced to retreat a few steps. At the right edge of my field of vision, I noticed Riothamus's Breton riders spill from around the fringe of the greenwood. In a show of great skill, the Bretons extended their line and thundered down on the rear of the unsuspecting Goths.

The right flank of the Goths, all heavy infantry, who had faced the men of Count Paul on our left, suddenly turned about to meet the new threat.

"Something is wrong", I shouted to Kursik to be heard above the din of battle. "How can they turn their back to the Romans?"

Count Paul's men did not push their advantage, and my first thought was that they were either exhausted, or expecting a trap.

But at the sound of the buccina, the men of Syagrius turned to face us, and fell upon our flank. For a spell I failed to believe my own eyes. Kursik grabbed the reins of my horse and pulled me back from the front rank.

"Axe", he boomed, and the bearded weapon found its way into my fist.

All around, Herulian lancers fell to the spears of Count Paul's footmen who had pushed deep into our flank.

Kursik pointed at the treeline to the rear. "It is our only hope", he shouted.

"Our way is blocked", I shouted in reply.

"Then cut a path with your blade", he said. In one fluid movement Kursik snatched his horn bow from its case, strung it, and took four arrows in his draw hand.

Trokondas would have been proud of me, I remember thinking. The men of Count Paul battled with the Herulians who wielded awkward long lances – weapons never intended for close combat. I had been trained to use the bearded axe from horseback, and my Damascus blade cut a bloody swathe through the enemy foot, who recoiled from the gore-covered apparition bearing down on them. From time to time their spears and swords breached my defences, but my excubitor armour turned the blades without fail.

We burst into the woods, with five of Syagrius's mounted spearmen thundering after us – foolishly pursuing a Hun with a bow in his hand. Kursik twisted his torso and sent five armour-piercing shafts at them, emptying their saddles in as many heartbeats.

"We have to go back for the erilar", I said once we were deep into the forest, and reined in my horse.

"He will be in the centre with Tribune Odovaker", the Hun replied. Without another word we spurred our horses back towards the mayhem.

We exited the treeline a few hundred paces to the east of where we had entered, right behind where we believed Abdarakos would be. The centre, where the heavily armoured Scirii's ranks had just broken, had descended into chaos. Not far from us, maybe fifty paces, Odovaker and Abdarakos still fought, surrounded by the tribune's hearthmen.

I kicked my tired mount to a gallop. Kursik rode at my side, and we forced our way through the flood of fleeing Scirii.

"It is over, we must flee", I shouted to Odovaker, who turned to face me.

"We can still win", Abdarakos boomed from close by, and in that moment I realised that they were not aware of the treachery of Count Paul.

"It is over", I shouted. "Count Paul has betrayed us."

Abdarakos had fought many battles in his long years. Most he had won, but not all, and he knew what had to be done.

"If we fall today", he boomed to a still defiant Odovaker, "who will avenge our betrayal?"

Chapter 36 – Count Paul (April 474 AD)

The old shaman stood at the prow of the longboat, his left arm wrapped around a wooden carving depicting a creature from the deep that I prayed only existed in the minds of men.

He raised an open palm, and the rowers shipped their oars without a sound. A heartbeat later the oak hull grated to a halt against the rough limestone of the river wall of Andecavus.

Abdarakos placed a hand on my shoulder. "Go with the gods, Ragnar", he growled.

I nodded, looped the length of knotted rope around my shoulders, and pressed my fingers into one of the large cracks where the wall had fallen into disrepair.

By the time my hand reached the top of the battlements, I was sweating profusely although the night was cold. I noticed the approach of a guard. As he passed, I silently swung onto the wall walk and grabbed him from behind, clasping my hand over his mouth. He struggled, but I was as strong as an ox and soon his body went limp.

I looped the rope around a merlon and allowed the loose end to fall to the boat, which was all but invisible given the overcast sky.

By the time that Beremud's head eventually appeared in a crenelation, I had already fitted the guard's clothes and armour. When my friend laid eyes on me, he nearly lost his purchase on the wall, but I grabbed his tunic and hauled him onto the walkway.

"Where do we go?" the big Goth whispered between gasps of breath once he had gained the safety of the battlements.

Earlier the same day, Beremud had abducted (or freed, as he liked to call it) a Goth kitchen slave while she collected water from the river. The terrified wench had provided Atakam with the layout of the interior of the fortress in exchange for her life and a promise of passage to the far bank.

I gestured to a door in the tower at the end of the rampart, feeling less confidence than that which I displayed to my companion.

We found the door unlocked and made our way down a musty stone stairway inside the tower to where another door gave access to a long, narrow passage dimly illuminated by oil lamps strategically placed in recesses along the wall.

"It leads to the quarters of the count", I said.

"Are you sure?" Beremud whispered.

299

"No", I replied and started down the passage which ended at another door at the far end.

The iron hinges of the door creaked, which provided the necessary heartbeat required for Beremud to conceal himself behind a stone pillar.

A guard, similarly attired, called out to me, his hand remaining on the knob of the door for much needed stability. "Like I've said before, Marius has just brought a fresh cask from the kitchens", he shouted in Latin with a slight, yet unmistakable slur of the tongue.

Unsure of what to do, I waved my hand in a dismissive gesture. "Suit yourself", the guard said and slammed the door shut. But then the hinges creaked again and his face appeared in the crack. "Seeing that you're not drinking, go and relieve Rufinus", he said. "The count asked for a guard at the door since he's got an important guest and all."

"Has he gone?" Beremud whispered twenty heartbeats later.

Since the guards seemed to be occupied with the cask of ale, I made my way towards the quarters of Count Paul without incident, Beremud following a couple of paces behind.

"I think it is around the next corner", I said.

An idea came to me. "Fall down", I told the big Goth, and gestured to the passage that would be in the line of sight of the guard. "Make sure that the guard can see both your feet."

"I'll do it", he scowled. "But this story stays inside the walls of this fort."

Beremud fell down heavily, his feet coming to rest in the passage in clear view of the door guard. Less than a heartbeat later I stepped around the corner, with my back half-turned to the hearthman of Count Paul, and waved him over, my blade in my hand.

When confronted with a situation like that, it is natural for one's attention to be focused on the threat, which in this case was the large prone barbarian sprawled on the flagstones. The guard drew his sword and poked Beremud in the side, like one would with a presumed-dead dog to determine whether it is alive or not.

My Goth friend cursed, but it was already too late for the unfortunate guard. Before he could jump back, or worse, stick his blade into my friend, the pommel of my sword slammed into his temple and he crumpled to the stone, on top of Beremud, who, predictably, cursed again.

Once we had dragged the guard into a doorway, we advanced to the grand double door. I took my sword in my fist and reached out to jerk open the door. But just as I was about to, I heard men conversing in Greek.

I immediately recognised the haughty tone so typical of the upper classes of the court of the City of Constantine. The men on the other side of the door spoke loudly, without fear of being overheard, as none other in Andecavus would even recognise high Greek, never mind understand it.

"Lord Syagrius is not the only one who has, er, reached out, to Caesar Leo", I heard the Greek emissary say.

I imagined Count Paul thinking on the words of the emperor's man while savouring a swallow of wine.

"Who else?" he asked.

"Lord Julius Nepos, the governor of Dalmatia, has been to the court of our lord recently", the Greek said.

"But Lord Syagrius visited the Great City only months ago", Count Paul replied. "And Emperor Leo gave him an undertaking. All my master had to do, apart from paying the gold, was to weaken the armies of Emperor Glycerius. We have held up our end of the bargain."

I heard the Greek issue a haughty snicker. "You have not heard, have you?" he asked.

"Heard what?" Paul replied.

"Old Emperor Leo has succumbed to a stomach ailment but two months ago", the Greek said. "His grandson Leo II, now rules in his stead. I am afraid that you have an agreement with a corpse."

A long silence ensued.

"But the boy is little older than a toddler", he said. "How can he rule the whole of the East?"

"The boy Leo has crowned his father, Zeno, as co-emperor", the emissary replied. "As we speak, Lord Julius Nepos is on his way to Rome to take his rightful place on the throne. But", the emissary added, "Caesar Zeno will be grateful if you supported Emperor Julius Nepos."

I heard the sound of a blade sliding from a scabbard. "My Lord Syagrius has given gold to the old man Leo", Count Paul hissed. "The Roman throne belongs to him."

It was time to act. I burst into the chamber only to find a blade buried up to the hilt in the gut of the Greek emissary. Count Paul, his fist still holding the sword, stared at me in confusion, and was about to admonish me when he realised that I was not the guard he had taken me for.

"You dare to enter the private room of the count, heathen?" he screamed while feverishly trying to free his blade stuck in the abdomen of the writhing emissary. I silently thanked Beremud for having the foresight of shutting the thick oak doors behind him.

I closed the gap between me and Count Paul and took what I was sent to retrieve.

"Better wrap it in his cloak first", Beremud said, his words no doubt backed by experience. "Or carry it yourself."

Chapter 37 – Boat Lord

I stood at the stern of the longboat, my right hand on the steering oar. The powerful strokes of the rowers propelled the ship downstream, towards the place where the Loire spills into the sea.

"So, Emperor Leo is dead", Abdarakos mused.

"I fear he is", I replied. "Finally Zeno will be able to pursue his own wicked agenda. I pray to the gods that Trokondas will be safe in that nest of vipers."

"When the boy Leo is older, he will get a mind of his own and temper Zeno's cravings", Abdarakos replied.

"If he gets older", Atakam said.

"Surely you do not believe that Zeno will harm his own son?" I asked.

Abdarakos did not offer a reply but pointed at a mast visible farther along the river. "Before Mourdagos had departed with his fleet, he told me to be careful. The Visigoths operate a fleet of ships along the coast. Sometimes they venture up the Loire. The Goths have taken over the fleet of the Romans which they use to chase away pirates."

"Are we pirates?" Kursik asked.

I tried to see my friend as an outsider would. A battle-hardened barbarian warrior, bristling with weapons, with a fierce, scarred, tattooed face. "I believe they will think us pirates", I replied earnestly.

The erilar ran his hand along the oak railing of the ship. "Mourdagos gave her to me after Count Paul bribed him with gold to leave Andecavus", he said. "She is as swift as the wind. He loaned me a boatload of his best men to man the oars."

"Where did Mourdagos go?" I asked.

"He is raiding the settlements along the coast", Abdarakos replied. "It might well be that he has returned north already."

We heeded the warning of the erilar and moored the boat in a small side channel in sight of the great walls of Roman Condevincum. The mouth of the Loire was a busy waterway and we decided that it would be best to exit the river under the cover of darkness, which, naturally, created another problem – we would require a helmsman familiar with the river.

We were not stupid enough to venture into the town during daylight, when all would recognise us for what we were, therefore we decided to wait for dusk to arrive.

"Any word of Odovaker?" I asked while we lounged on the deck in the afternoon sun.

"Yesterday I spoke with a trader on his way west from Burgundia", Atakam said. "He mentioned that Odovaker and Riothamus had arrived in Burgundia and are under the protection of Gundobad, their king. I believe that Odovaker will return to Italia as soon as the passes are traversable."

"Odovaker has become a man of reputation", Abdarakos said. "Even the recent defeat against Euric has enhanced his esteem among the warriors. All know that it is the treachery of Count Paul and Syagrius that is to blame."

"And Childeric?" I asked.

"He did not flee the field of battle like a coward, but led his men to safety. His brave and honourable actions saved the lives of many", Abdarakos said. "I believe that he has the makings to be a great king of the Franks, and a thorn in the side of Syagrius the oathbreaker."

* * *

Come late afternoon, Beremud and I made our way towards the town.

The gods sent a light drizzle to aid us in our mission, as none found it strange that the hoods of cloaks were pulled down over our faces. We were not ignorant enough to venture through the gates of the town, but found a drinking establishment inside the sprawling settlement abutting the massive stone walls.

There were still many unoccupied tables inside the 'Thirsty Mackerel', a drinking hole near the river port. We chose a spot close to the door and took our seats. Within ten heartbeats a comely serving girl scurried over.

Beremud had a way with women and smiled at the dark-haired girl. "Are you the owner of this establishment?" he asked earnestly.

"No, good sir", she replied, "I work here for a copper a day and a decent hot meal."

The big Goth held out his open hand and to my surprise the girl put her hand in his. Beremud turned her palm to face upwards and placed a silver coin inside.

"I'm not that type of woman", she said.

"I can see that", he replied. "It is a gift."

The girl blushed and walked away, only to return a few moments later. "I forgot to take your order", she said. She did not even afford me a second glance, having eyes only for Beremud.

Not long after, she arrived with two mugs of ale and two bowls of steaming fish stew. It did not come as a surprise that, unlike my bowl, Beremud's was filled to the brim.

In any event, the pottage turned out to be delicious and the ale of surprisingly high quality. After we had finished our second bowl of stew and fifth mug of ale, Beremud waved the barmaid over, who scrambled to serve her favourite customer.

He leaned in towards the girl, who reciprocated. "I am in need of a river pilot, lady", he said. "One who will be willing and able to guide us through the shallows of the mouth during the hours of darkness."

"One has to be careful", she whispered, keeping her voice barely audible. "There are many unsavoury types that use the river, but I can see that you are a proper gentleman. My father knows the mouth like the back of his hand", she said, and smiled sweetly at my big friend.

"But", she said with a mock frown, "he will need a hostage to guarantee his safe return."

Needless to say – Beremud volunteered.

* * *

The old man eyed us warily, clearly reluctant to step aboard, his hand on the hilt of what I assumed was a fish knife.

"My daughter told me you are gentlemen traders", he said in peasant Latin. "But to me you look like them Saxon raiders."

Abdarakos handed him three gold coins.

"But you know what they say about looks, eh - they can be deceiving", he said, offered a gap-toothed smile, and proceeded to step onto the oak planking.

The barmaid had not lied to us about the skills of her father. The old fisherman guided us around unseen sandbanks and submerged rocks that often scraped the bottom of the hull.

Just after the middle hour of the night the man announced that we had arrived in open water. He proceeded to guide us to a sandy cove where his daughter and the hostage would be waiting.

I must say that it did cross my mind that Beremud could have eloped with the girl, but my fears were laid to rest when the hulking hostage appeared over the rise of the dunes, arm-in-arm with the daughter of the old helmsman.

Beremud waded through the shallows and climbed aboard while the pilot returned to his daughter.

I realised that something was amiss with my friend, who immediately sought out Abdarakos.

"I wish to take the girl with me", he said.

It was the last thing that the erilar had expected. It was one of the few, if not the only time, my grandfather was at a loss for words.

"Go get the girl", Atakam answered on behalf of Abdarakos, "it is the will of the gods."

* * *

We spent the night anchored just off the beach in the calm water. When dusk arrived, we broke our fast and ventured out into the open ocean.

Beremud's woman, whose name was Maela, proved to be a godsent, just like Atakam had predicted. Once we were clear of the coast, she spoke with my grandsire. "Lord", she said in her peasant Latin, "we have seen many Goth boats sail past the town in the last days. They were all heading out to sea, lord."

We heeded the girl's warning and remained vigilant. All of us watching the horizon for any sign of the Goth fleet.

But again, it was the girl who first spotted the danger. "There", she shouted and pointed at three masts barely visible above a rocky inlet to the east.

In response Abdarakos pushed the steering oar to the right and the prow of the longboat came around to the west, headed out to the open ocean. Not a hundred heartbeats passed when three masts, under full sail, appeared on the horizon ahead of us.

"I spent many years serving in the bar", the girl told Abdarakos. "I listened to the talk of the seamen, lord. The Goths hunt in packs. Three ships close to shore, three ships in the open ocean and three ships on both sides of the river mouth. We are like a mackerel caught in a net, lord."

The erilar grunted his acknowledgement of Maela's words, but pulled on the steering oar nonetheless, aiming the prow of the ship towards the gap between the converging group of Goth ships, in an attempt to escape towards the north.

We all knew what would likely happen, but hoped that the girl had been wrong. Our worst fears were confirmed when Kursik pointed at a single mast on the northern horizon, blocking our escape. Soon the single ship was joined by two more. We had become the proverbial mackerel, just like Maela had predicted.

"Our only chance is to break through their cordon", Abdarakos said. "Their ships are under sail, which makes them more difficult to steer." He slapped the top of the wooden railing. "This is a sturdy ship. We will meet them prow to prow and see if they can be outmanoeuvred."

The erilar indicated one of the Goth ships, which was still two miles distant, and turned the prow of the longboat towards it.

Like a net to catch fish, the Goth ships spread out on the horizon. We knew that there was little chance of evading the enemy, but the presence of Abdarakos inspired us, and served to put iron into our hearts.

So fixed was our attention on the Goth boat, that we failed to notice the multitude of warships behind it.

A rower spied the ships. "Look to the north", he shouted, "we are doomed."

Abdarakos scowled at the warrior, but did not reprimand him because he knew that the man spoke the truth. First, ten hulls appeared from over the horizon, then more, all bearing down on us like wolves on their prey.

My grandsire grabbed me by the shoulder. "Although we are doomed", he whispered, "we will still try. I will not spend my last days on bent knees as a slave in Euric's court."

I went to the prow of the ship, joining Boarex and Kursik. To my surprise they had not strung their bows, but stood with battle-axes in both hands. I took my bearded axe in my right fist, while my left hand found the hilt of my dagger.

"May you have a good death", Kursik said, his eyes fixed on the nearing enemy, and his lips curled up in a snarl.

"I have often wondered how it will end", Boarex said, and with a swooping motion of his axe gestured to the wide-open sea. He drew a deep breath and exhaled slowly. "And I thank the gods because it cannot be better than this."

We drew closer to the Goth boat, whose prow rose and fell as it surmounted the onrushing waves, reminding me of a horse at full gallop.

I steeled myself for the impact.

But an arrow arced high from one of the boats behind and descended onto the deck of the Goth ship, slamming into the skull of the steersman. The boat swerved from our path as the man at the helm slumped onto the oar.

For the first time we were afforded a clear view of the approaching ships. At the prow of the leading longboat stood a bear of a man, one hand draped around the carved beast's head, his chain and scale glittering in the late morning light.

The Boat Lord had come to the land of the Goths.

To be continued...

Historical Note – Main Characters

Heruli and their companions

- **Ragnaris** is a Hun name with Germanic origins. He is a
  fictional character, following the journey of the Heruli
  through the fifth century AD.
- **Ildiko's** name is recorded in history. She was the bride of
  Attila and probably of Germanic origin.
- The Heruli family and friends of Ragnaris are all fictional.
  That includes **Abdarakos**, **Mourdagos**, **Sigizan**,
  Atakam, **Leodis, Kursik, Beremud** and **Asbadus.**
- **Rodolph** became the king of the Heruli during this time.
  It is not known who preceded him, but John the Deacon
  mentions that he was the last of their kings.
- Flavius Odoacer/**Odovaker/Ottoghar** was presumably a
  Scirii chieftain, who became a leading general in the West
  Roman foederati. He is mentioned as the king of the
  Heruli.

Romans

- **Leo the Thracian** was the East Roman emperor from 457
  AD to 474 AD. It is said that he was a Bessian.

- **Flavius Zeno** was an Isaurian and reigned as Byzantine Emperor from 474 to 491 AD. (Albeit with a short interruption during 475/6 AD). His birth name was **Tarasis** Kodisa Rousombladadiotes.

- Flavius Ardabur **Aspar** was of Alanic-Gothic descent. From 424 AD until his death in 471 AD he was the real power behind the purple of the Eastern Roman Empire. He was an Arian Christian, and therefore not eligible to be emperor (some say that it was because he was of barbarian stock). **Ardabur** and **Patricius** were his sons.

- The name **Trokondas** is not fictional. Trokondas (or Trocundes) was an Isaurian general, famous in history with his brother **Illus**. Trokondas was often an ally of Zeno and often an enemy.

- **Sidonius Apollinaris** was a high born Roman and the bishop of Clermont. He was more than just a bishop and had a hand in organising the defences of the ailing Roman Empire in Gaul. Much of our knowledge of the history of this period relies on his writings.

Men of the tribes

- **Attila** was the king or khan of the Huns.
- **Theodemir** was the king of the Ostrogoths and the father of **Theoderic the Great**.

317

- **Vidimir** was the brother of Theodemir, a king of a portion of the Ostrogoths. His son was also called **Vidimir**.

- **Geiseric** was the king of the Vandals, a Germanic tribe which, together with a grouping of Alans, conquered North Africa and established the Vandal Kingdom. Their ships caused havoc in the Mediterranean through piracy and coastal raids during the second half of the fifth century. It is said that he was a very clever and resourceful man.

- **Ferderuchus** and **Feva** (Feletheus was also known as Feva) were the sons of **Flaccitheus**, King of the Rugii. After Flaccitheus's death, Feva became king. Feva was married to an Ostrogoth woman by the name of **Gisa**, close family of Theodemir's.

- **Aldihoc** was the king of the Lombards during the middle of the fifth century AD. His son **Godehoc** succeeded him somewhere around 480 AD.

- **Euric** was the king of the Visigoths from 466 AD to 484 AD.

- **Childeric** was the king of the Franks during this period. He is believed to be the son of **Merovech**, father of the Merovingian dynasty.

- **Riothamus** was a Breton/British leader who fought against the Visigoths in Gaul. Some identify him with (the legendary?) King Arthur.

318

The Svear and Gautar

- **Unni** and **Runa** are fictional. They represent the Svear people and their agrarian culture.
- **Aun the Old** and his son **Egil** (Ogentheow) were legendary kings of the Svear.
- **Haecyn** and **Hygelac** were both legendary kings of the Gautar.

Historical Note – Storyline

The Heruli in Scandinavia

Archaeological evidence, especially the princely horse equipment found at Sösdala, indicate that during the fifth century AD, Eastern European horse warriors arrived on the shores of Scandinavia.

In his famous work, the *Heimskringla, Snorri Sturluson* tells of Odin, a great warlord, who arrived from the lands of the East. Snorri mentions that Odin was superior to the locals in many ways and imparted his skills and customs. In later years, these early rulers were revered as gods.

I choose to believe that the Heruli (which had lived under Hunnic rule for long) were the ones responsible for the Eastern European influence. Their trek to Scandinavia is recorded by *Procopius*. It has been suggested that they settled amongst the people and became a military elite. The Scandinavian term *jarl* (equivalent to the British earl or duke) is said to be linked to the Heruli and the *erilaR* inscriptions found on elder futhark runestones.

The first part of the book where Ragnar arrives back in Scandinavia is an attempt to create a scenario of the initial contact between the Heruli and the indigenous tribes.

* * *

There is much speculation about the nature of the relationship between the Svear and the Geats (Gautar), the two major tribes of the land which is called Sweden nowadays.

The epic poem of Beowulf, set in early sixth century Scandinavia, is one of the few sources that sheds some light on these times. Beowulf, a Geat, travelled to the land of the Danes to lend a hand to their king, Hrothgar, who had assisted Beowulf's father in earlier years. I relied on this to assume that the Geats had come to some arrangement of peace with the Danes during the latter part of the fifth century.

The *Historia Norwegiae* and the *Ynglinga saga* by *Snorri Sturluson* served as inspiration and reference. The skaldic poem, *Ynglingatal,* is cited by Sturluson as one of the main sources of the saga. Sturluson's work is dated to around 1225 AD and the original poem to 872 AD. **I must stress that I did not attempt to follow the history contained in the legendary sagas to the letter, but used it as inspiration to depict the arrival of the Heruli.**

According to the sagas, Aun the Old was king of the Svear during the fifth century. He sacrificed his sons to the gods in order to gain old age. The people refused to allow his last remaining son, Egil Vendelcrow (Ogentheow), to be sacrificed.

Procopius describes the Heruli custom of killing a man when he becomes old or infirm. It was deemed honourable for the wife of the man to hang herself above the grave of her husband.

During this time in history the burial customs of the Swedes changed. The mounds at Uppsala, which bear many similarities to the kurgans of the Eurasian Steppes, are seen for the first time. The oldest mound at Uppsala is known as Aun's mound which is dated to the fifth century AD, the time that the Heruli is believed to have settled in Scandinavia.

According to the sagas, Egil Vendelcrow (Ogentheow) succeeded Aun the Old.

During the reign of Egil, Hrethel was the king of the Geats. Hrethel died of grief when his son Herebeald was killed by his own brother Haecyn during a hunting accident. Haecyn then acceded to the throne. Sad to say, but it does sound like a conspiracy.

Haecyn then attacked the Svear, kidnapped Egil's queen, and stole her treasure. Egil pursued Haecyn to a hillfort called

Hrefnesholt. At the fort, the queen was rescued. Haecyn was killed in the battle, but the treasure lost.

Hygelac, Haecyn's brother, then became king of the Geats. Hygelac features in the poem Beowulf, and is said to have died in 521 AD.

According to the *Ynglinga saga* and the *Historia Norwegiae,* Egil was killed by the horns of a bull. According to *Beowulf,* Egil was slain by Eofor, a hearthman of Hygelac. An interesting theory draws a comparison between these two stories. Apparently, the words of the sagas translate to the 'sword of the snout' rather than horns of a bull. Also, Eofor means boar. I took the liberty to interpret this that Egil was killed in battle by a *svinfylking* (boar snout) formation, which was employed to break through enemy ranks.

Egil reigned for another three years after killing the king of the Gautar, but I had no patience to put up with him for so long.

Othere succeeded to the throne. He was the son of Egil, but I do not know whether he was a bastard or not.

* * *

At this point, Ragnar leaves the far shores of Scandza and returns to the lands controlled, or influenced, by Rome.

Things had not gone the way of the Western Empire for many years, but during 472 AD things took a turn for the worse. Relations between Emperor Anthemius and his high general, the Germanic kingmaker Ricimer, deteriorated to the point of civil war. Ricimer died soon after he had the emperor executed, leaving Olybrius as emperor. Before the end of 472 AD Olybrius also died. Early in 473 AD, Ricimer's successor, Prince Gundobad of the Burgundians, appointed Glycerius as emperor. The high general left Italy soon after to become the king of his people after his father, Gundioc, passed away.

At this time the Ostrogoths lived in Pannonia, to the east of Noricum. They had been allowed to settle in Pannonia, a part of the Eastern Empire, shortly after the death of Attila. But during 473 AD, the Goths became restless. They had exhausted the resources of Pannonia and the surrounding lands, and were starting to suffer from famine. They implored their chieftains, Theodemir and Vidimir, to lead them somewhere where they could sustain themselves through plunder. Eventually Theodemir split from Vidimir. Theodemir invaded the Eastern Empire and Vidimir set out to attack the Western Roman Empire.

Eugippius recorded the life of Saint Severinus of Noricum. In chapter five he mentions an incident where the Ostrogoths capture a group of men affiliated with the Rugii. Severinus warns Flaccitheus not to pursue them: *"If thou follow them,"* he said, *"thou wilt be slain. Take heed; cross not the stream; be not taken unawares and overcome by the triple ambush which has been prepared for thee!"* I used this as the basis for Ragnar's adventure on his return from Theodemir's camp.

During this time the wolves started to descend on the Western Empire. Vidimir and his Ostrogoths invaded Italy where they suffered a number of defeats, and Vidimir was killed. Emperor Glycerius bribed the Goths with gifts of food and clothing, dissuading them from further hostilities. The Ostrogoths under Vidimir's son (also called Vidimir) were allowed safe passage to Gaul to join their kin, the Visigoths.

At this time the Lombards are mentioned as being tributary to the Heruli. This means that the Heruli must have subjugated the Lombards some time after the death of Attila. The battle between the Lombards and the Heruli (aided by Ottoghar) is my invention, as no account of it is recorded in history. Ottoghar or Flavius Odovaker is (amongst other) referred to as the king of the Heruli. I used this battle as his rise to become war leader (king in all but name) of the Heruli.

* * *

Our attention now turns to the happenings in Gaul.

Euric, the king of the Visigoths, who resided in the Iberian Peninsula, had been conquering Gaul piecemeal since 469 AD. During 473/475 AD, sensing the weakness of the Western Empire, he invaded Italy. The Visigoth army was defeated and its general, Vincentius, killed by Roman 'dukes', whose names, Alla and Sindila, hint at a barbarian heritage. Some believe that they were Odovaker's men. I believe that the battle must have taken place somewhere in the vicinity of modern Turin. Based on references from the *Notitia Dignitatum*, it is accepted that a large group of Alans had been settled at Pollentium, thirty miles south of Turin. I have taken the liberty to assume that Alla and Sindila were Alanic dukes settled in the area.

The tale that Odovaker weaves concerning Ricimer, is close to the truth. A school of thought exists that believes Ricimer killed Emperor Majorian because his expansionist policies had started to endanger the survival of the Empire.

Goar, Sangiban and Beogar were all Alani leaders. I invented the fact that Sangiban usurped Goar, although it is possible, as Goar

326

disappears from the records during the time that Sangiban appears. There is no evidence that Beogar was the son of Goar, although, again, it is possible.

* * *

At this stage our heroes cross the Alps into Gaul.

My inspiration for Odovaker's excursion into Gaul is the following extract from the English translation of *Gregory of Tours', Historia Francorum:*

> *"Odoacer came with his Saxons to Angers. This was the time when a great epidemic ravaged the population. Aegidius died leaving a son called Syagrius. After his death Odoacer took hostages from Angers and other places. The Britons were driven out of Bourges by the Goths and many of them were killed at Bourg-de-Deols. Count Paul led Romans and Franks in a campaign against the Goths and carried off plunder. Odoacer came to Angers. The next day King Childeric arrived and took the city after Count Paul had been killed."*

In addition to *Gregory of Tours, Sidonius Apollinaris* as well as *Jordanes,* sheds light on the happenings in Gaul around this time.

The Saxons lived in close proximity to the Western Heruli. To some, the two groups may have been indistinguishable. My interpretation is that Odovaker visited Angers accompanied by a warband of Heruli.

The main players in Gaul during this time need their own special introduction:

- **Childeric**, the son of Merovech (from there the Merovingian dynasty), was a Frankish king occupying the northern part of Roman Gaul.
- **Riothamus** – He is believed to be a Breton war leader from Armorica allied to the Romans. His name/title translates to 'great lord', but his real name might have been different. He is identified with (the legendary) British King, Arthur. Riothamus was defeated by Euric in a major battle sometime between 471 and 475 AD. His warband might have included Alans. These East European horse warriors were settled in the area of Armorica by command of General Aetius, the Roman who defeated/stalemated Attila the Hun. It is possible that Riothamus was of Alanic descent.

328

- A large part of Northern Gaul was called the Kingdom of the Soissons. This was ruled over by **Syagrius**, who insisted to be referred to as a Roman governor. **Count Paul** was a Roman warlord, possibly affiliated with Syagrius.

Glycerius, who had been abandoned by his high general, Gundobad, did not have the support of the Eastern Empire, which was under the de facto rule of Zeno after Leo the Thracian passed away in January 474 AD.

In the spring of 474 AD, Zeno sent his chosen man, Julius Nepos, to Italy at the head of a fleet. At their arrival, a powerless Glycerius abdicated in favour of Nepos.

Some believe that Syagrius wished for Zeno to support his claim to the Western throne, but Zeno favoured Nepos.

Historical Note – Random Items

- Ragnar's carvings are inspired by the *Eggja runestone*, line two: *"This stone the runemaster sprinkled with blood, scraped with the blood the oarlock in the worn-out boat. As whom came the army god with the boat here to the Goth's land? As the fish, swimming out of the horror river, as the bird ... crowing."*

- The mid-winter sacrifices at Uppsala were held once every nine years, but due to the way the ancients counted, it took place every eighth year. In 468 AD the full moon, which coincided with the day of sacrifice, occurred on 26 February. The German missionary, Adam of Bremen, provided detail on these sacrifices around 1075 AD.

- Sigizan makes a boast that he is used to enduring worse cold. Winter nights of -40 degrees Celsius (-40 degrees Fahrenheit) is common on the Eastern Eurasian Steppes, while the temperature in Stockholm seldom drops below -15 degrees Celsius (5 degrees Fahrenheit).

- The Mora stone was similar in many ways to the Scottish stone of destiny. It was used in the coronation ceremony of ancient Swedish kings. During the war of 1515 AD the Mora stone was destroyed by the Danes. There is no surviving record detailing the inscription on the stone.

- *Mora* (singular *mor*) means 'dense forests on damp land'.
- Of the Viking ring forts excavated to date, the earliest are dated to around 800 AD. Having said that, excavations are under way at the ring fort at *Sandy borg* on the west coast of Öland, Sweden. This ring fort dates back to 480 AD. I could not help but notice the similarities between the layout of the ringforts and Roman marching camps.
- Oddvar's village I placed in the area of Nykoping, close to the area known as Kolmarden, which was the war-torn frontier between the Svear and the Geats. The Kolmarden area was heavily forested and rocky. In times of old it was seen as an obstacle when travelling by land.
- Mount Vesuvius, which destroyed Pompeii, erupted some time during 472 AD. Ash fell from the sky as far as Constantinople in the East.
- Wild boar weighing 770 lbs have been recorded, although not in Sweden, where they became extinct in the 18th century. They were reintroduced to the wild (by accident) when some escaped from enclosures. They spread rapidly throughout the country. Today their population is estimated at 150 000. In captivity, boars have lived up to twenty years.
- Corpse-sea is a kenning for blood. Whale-path or whale-road is a kenning for sea.

331

- Verina and Emperor Leo I had a third child in 463 AD. The child apparently died when he was five months old. I invented the link to *Justin I* to spice up the story. *Justin I* started his career as a swineherd in Dardania and managed to get recruited into the excubitors. His amazing feat moved me to speculation.

- Competent rowers are able to manage sixty nautical miles a day at sea. I believe the ancients were tougher, so I credited them with eighty nautical miles (ninety miles) per day.

- The Anemoi was a group of wind deities in Greek mythology. Each wind direction had its own god. Notus was the god of the south wind which brought the bad weather of late summer.

- *Hippocrates* is credited with the aphorism: *"Those diseases which medicines do not cure, iron cures; those which iron cannot cure, fire cures; and those which fire cannot cure, are to be reckoned wholly incurable."*

- The Elbe is a tidal river. Near Hamburg the water level differs by a mean of 3.66 meters between low and high tide. The tidal current of the flood tide near Hamburg runs at 2.5 knots.

- The meeting between Abdarakos and Aldihoc was modelled on a meeting between the Lombards and the Gepids which happened fifty years later.

- The duel between Ragnar and the Lombard champion is inspired by the single combat between Coccas and Anzalas in the Battle of Taginae fought between the Ostrogoths and Byzantium eighty years later.

- Abdarakos's description of the battle of the Catalaunian Plains is my spin on the actual happenings. The Alans were arrayed directly opposite Attila's forces and the two sides fought each other to a standstill. The Visigoths (Roman allies) were arrayed against the Ostrogoths (Attila's allies). The Visigoths broke the Ostrogoth line and fell on the flank of Attila's oathsworn. That night Thorismund, the prince of the Visigoths, 'mistakenly' ended up inside Attila's camp (really?). The next day his father, the Visigoth king, was found dead and although Thorismund beseeched Aetius to attack Attila's camp, the Roman general refused. It is generally accepted that Aetius withdrew because he feared that the Goths would turn on him if Attila were killed.

- The meeting on the road between Abdarakos and Sindila is modelled on the meeting between St. Germanicus who confronted the Alani warlord, Goar, on the road to

333

Armorica. His courage gained him respect in the eyes of the barbarian chieftain and their encounter ended in peaceful talks.

- During the second half of the third century AD the military equipment and fighting styles of the Roman army began to change. Oval shields replaced the old scutum, the gladius lengthened, spears evolved and cavalry became more popular. Some historians believe that the evidence points towards cavalry, especially mounted lancers, being used to break massed infantry ranks.

Historical Note – Place Names

City of Constantine – later known as Constantinople, then Istanbul, the capital of Turkey.

Runaville (fictional name) – Area of Herrhamra, Sweden.

Old Uppsala – Gamla Uppsala, Sweden, north of Stockholm.

The camp of the Boat Heruli – halfway between Hamburg and Lubeck, Germany. This is believed to be inside the ancient homeland of the Saxons, but there is a blurred line between them and the Heruli. Some believe that Herulians were part of the Saxons that invaded Britain.

The Gautar fort where Haecyn was killed – near Arkosund, Sweden. (This differs from the historical records.)

The Elbe River valley where the bear was killed by wolves – Valley of the Labe, near Děčín, Czechia, fifty miles north of Prague.

The great hall of King Flaccitheus of the Rugii – I have placed this just south of Ceske Budejovice on the Vitava, Czechia.

The camp of Theodemir's Goths in Roman Pannonia – near Vienna, Austria.

Commagenis in Roman Noricum – Tulln, Austria.

The place in Rugiland where Vidimir sets up an ambush for Flaccitheus – Göllitzhof region, Austria.

Budorigum on the Amber Road – Wroclaw, Poland.

Battle near the Moravian Gate (The Amber Gate) – Vicinity of Hranice, Czechia.

Augusta Taurinorum – Turin, Italy.

Averna (Old Roman Augusto Nemetum) – Modern day Clermont-Ferrand, France.

Andecavus – Angers, France.

Avaricum – Bourges, France.

Argentomagus – Saint Marcel, France.

Dolensus (Deols) – a suburb of Chateauroux, France.

Condevincum on the Loire – Nantes, France.

Author's Note

I trust that you have enjoyed the third book in the **erilaR** series.

My aim is to be as historically accurate as possible, but I am sure that I inadvertently miss the target from time to time, in which case I apologise to the purists among my readers.

Kindly take the time to provide a rating and/or a review.

I will keep you updated via my blog with regards to the progress on the fourth book in the series.

Feel free to contact me any time via my website. I will respond.

www.HectorMillerBooks.com

Other books by the same author:

erilaR Series

- Part 1 – Stranger from Another Land
- Part 2 – Blood of the Khan
- Part 3 – War God from the Sea

The Thrice Named Man Series

- Book I – Scythian
- Book II – Legionary

- Book III – Sasanian
- Book IV – Transsilvanian
- Book V – Goth
- Book VI – Roman
- Book VII – Illyrian
- Book VIII – Roxolani

Printed in Great Britain
by Amazon

65028380R00203